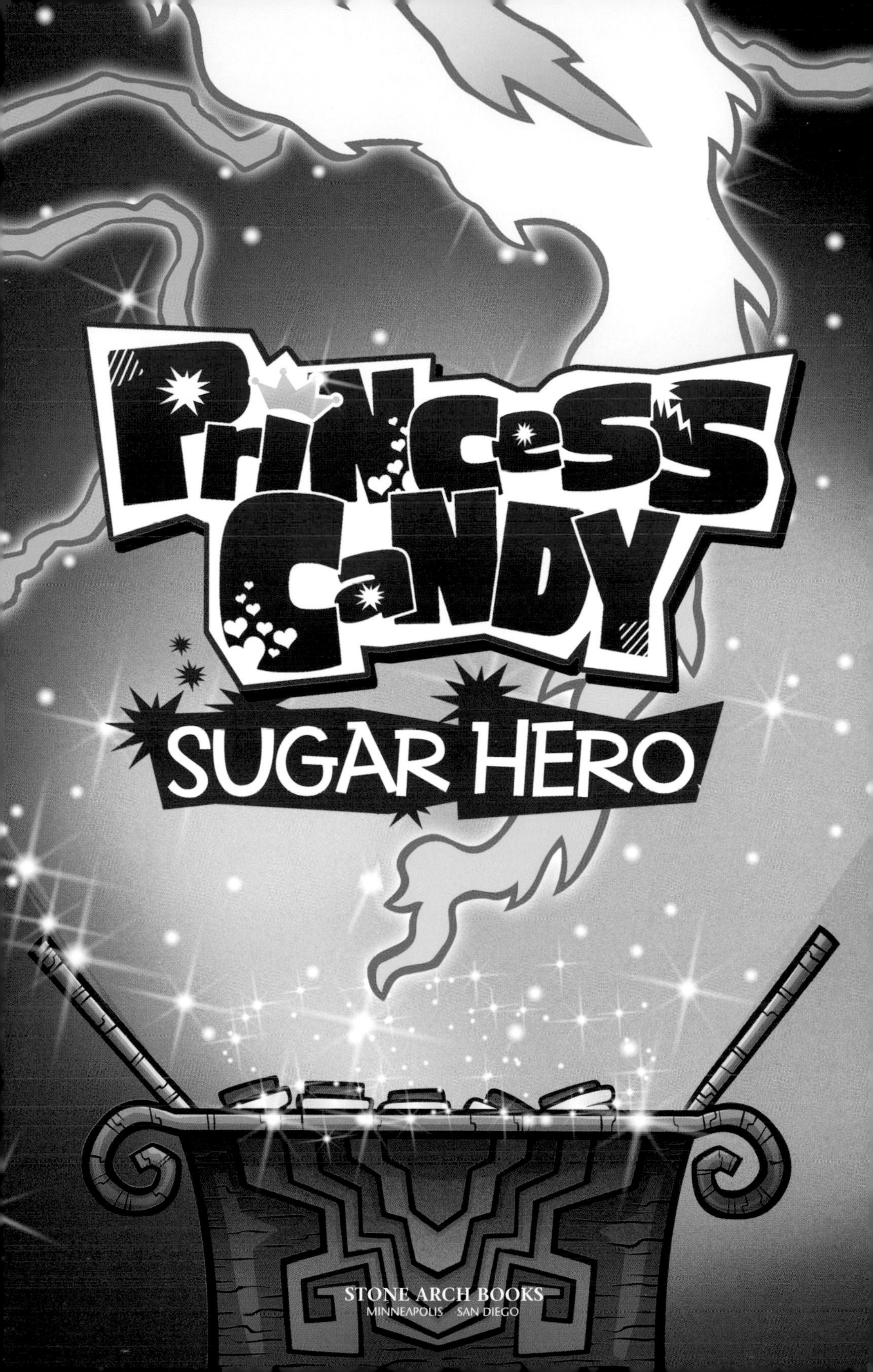
PRINCESS CANDY
SUGAR HERO
STONE ARCH BOOKS
MINNEAPOLIS SAN DIEGO

Graphic Sparks are published by Stone Arch Books,
A Capstone Imprint
151 Good Counsel Drive, P.O. Box 669
Mankato, Minnesota 56002
www.capstonepub.com

Library of Congress Cataloging-in-Publication Data

Dahl, Michael.
  Sugar hero / by Michael Dahl ; illustrated by Jeff Crowther.
    p. cm. -- (Graphic sparks. Princess Candy)
  ISBN 978-1-4342-1587-1 (lib. bdg.)
  ISBN 978-1-4342-2801-7 (pbk.)
  1. Graphic novels. [1. Graphic novels. 2. Superheroes--Fiction. 3.
Schools--Fiction.] I. Crowther, Jeff, ill. II. Title.
  PZ7.7.D34Su 2010
  741.5'973--dc22
                              2009011407

Summary: On Halo Nightly's eleventh birthday, her Aunt Pandora gives
her a collection of jars filled with brightly colored candies. Soon she
learns that the candies give her the incredible powers of nature.
Halo uses the powers to combat Doozie Hiss, a rival student with
superpowered hair.

Creative Director: Heather Kindseth
Designer: Brann Garvey

Printed in the United States of America in Stevens Point, Wisconsin.
032011
006139R

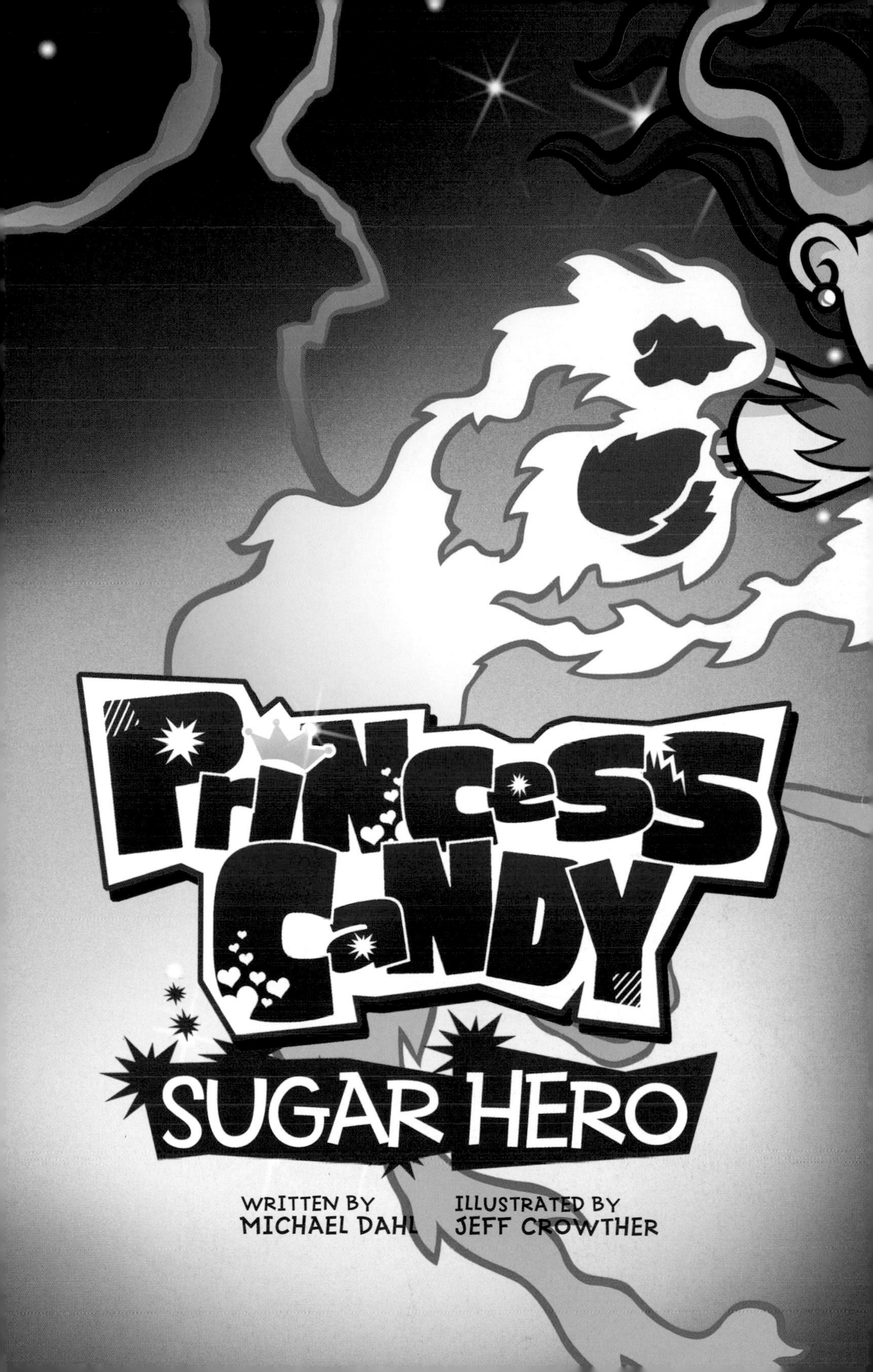
PRINCESS CANDY
SUGAR HERO
WRITTEN BY
MICHAEL DAHL
ILLUSTRATED BY
JEFF CROWTHER

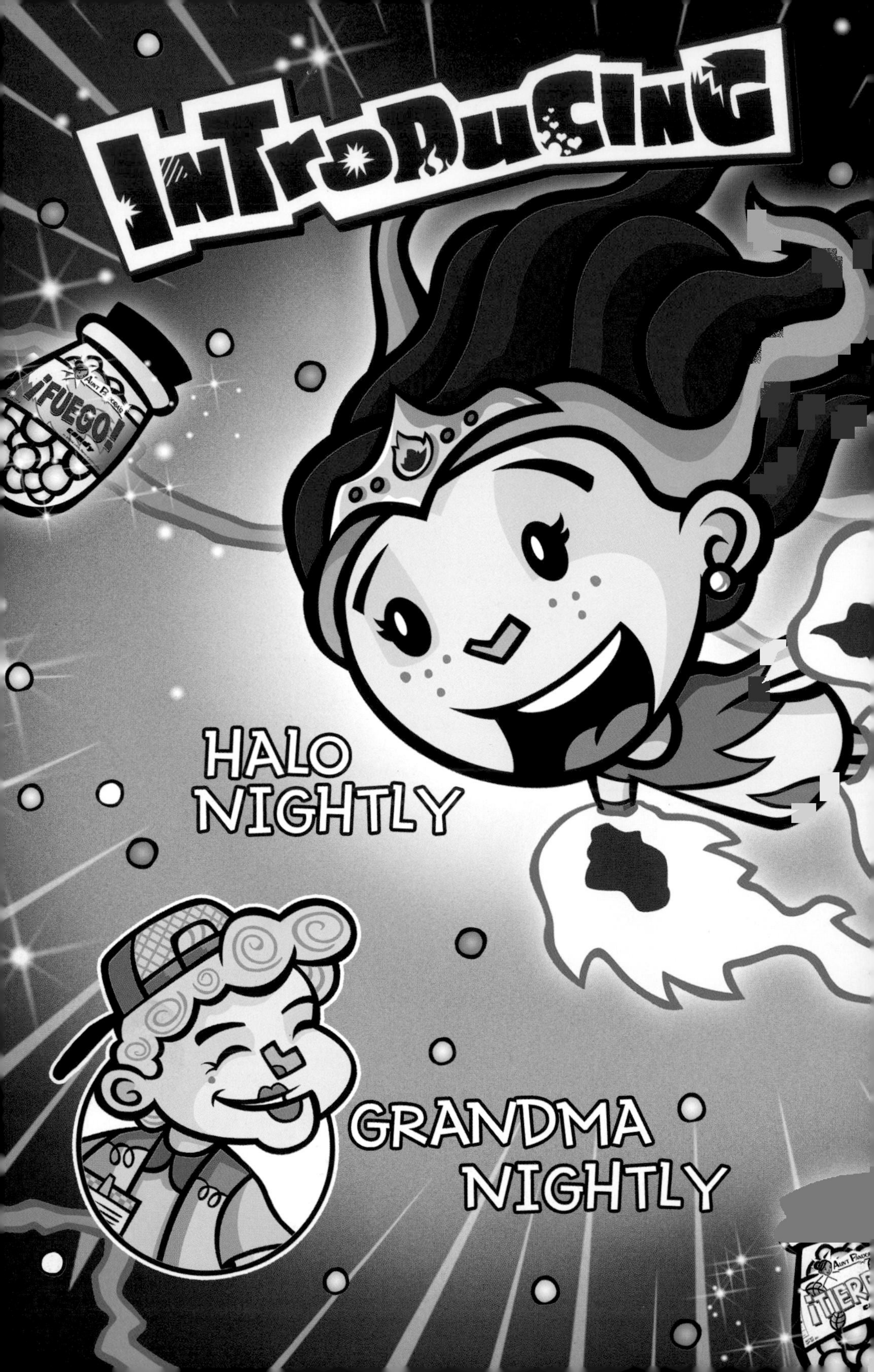
INTRODUCING
HALO NIGHTLY
GRANDMA NIGHTLY
¡FUEGO!

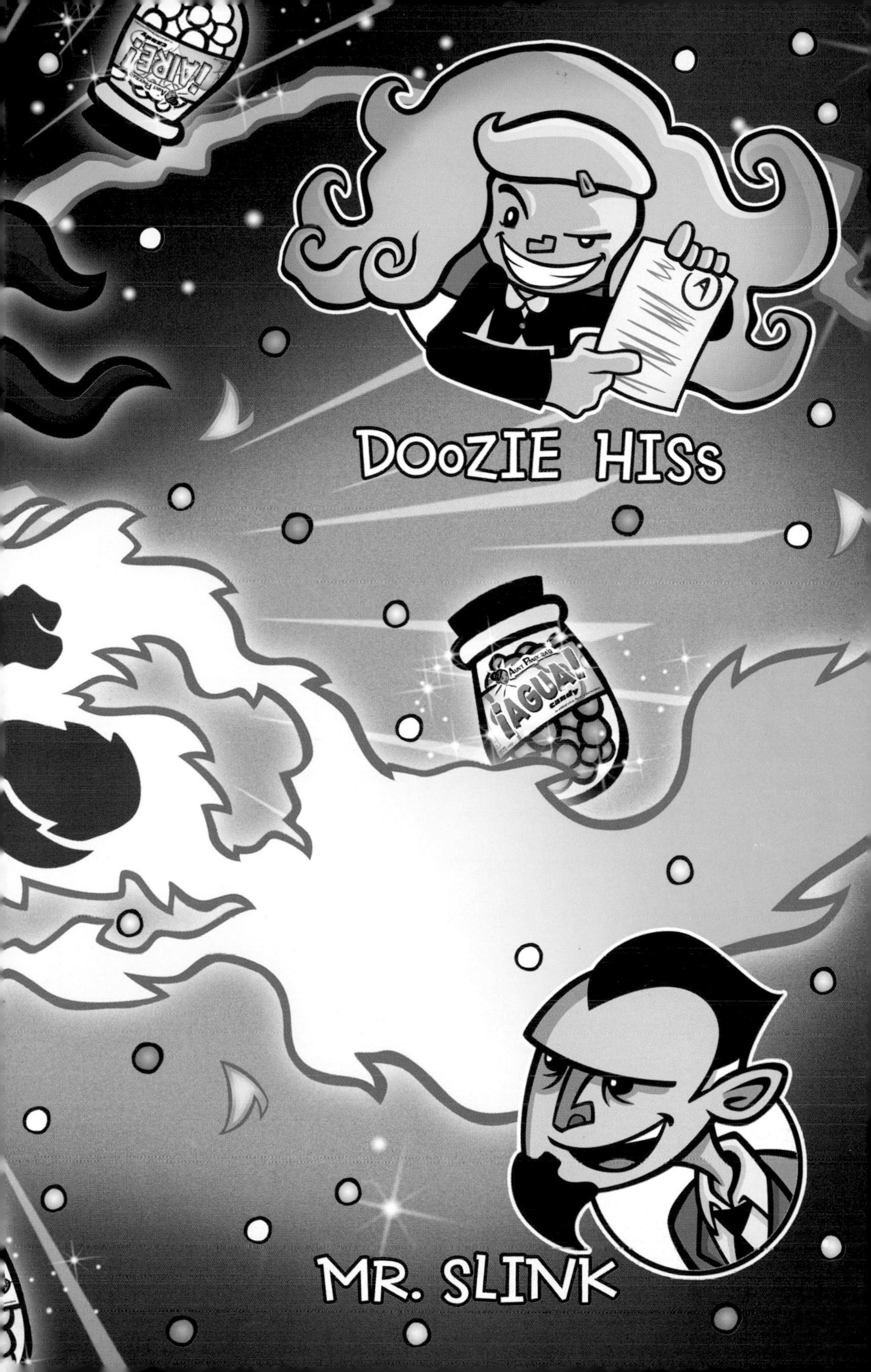
¡AIRE!
DOOZIE HISS
¡AGUA!
MR. SLINK

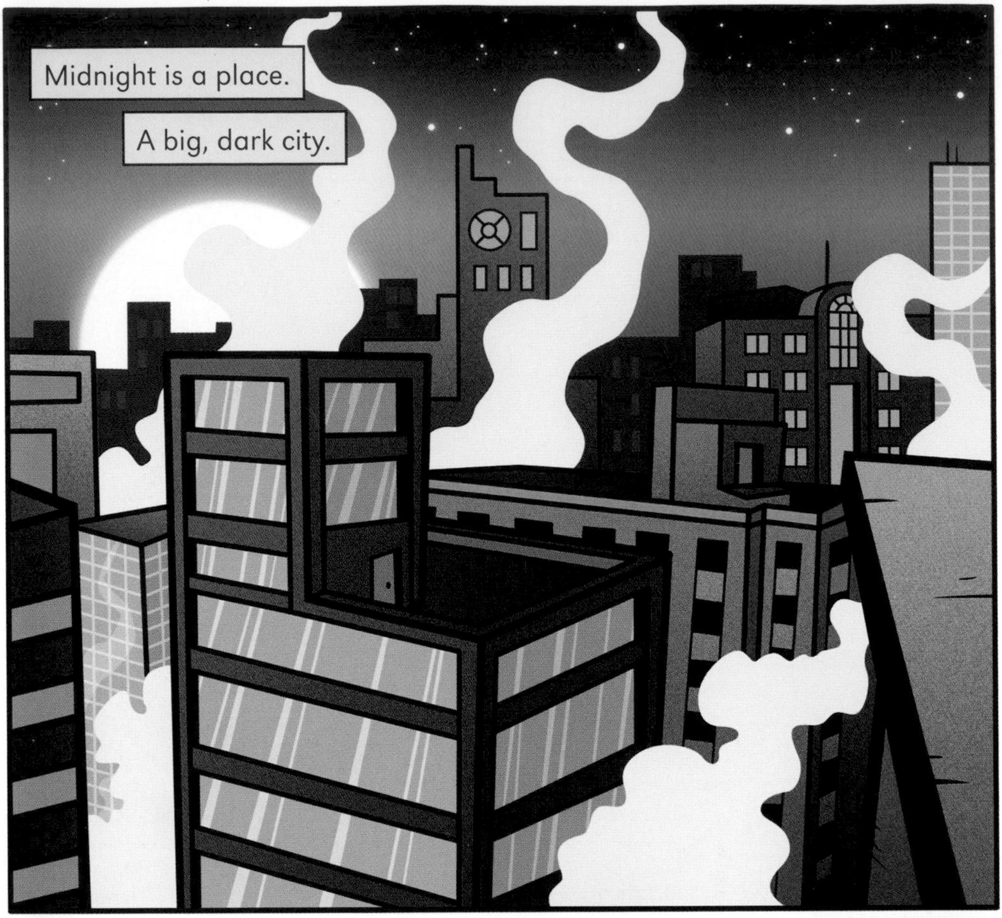
Midnight is a place.
A big, dark city.

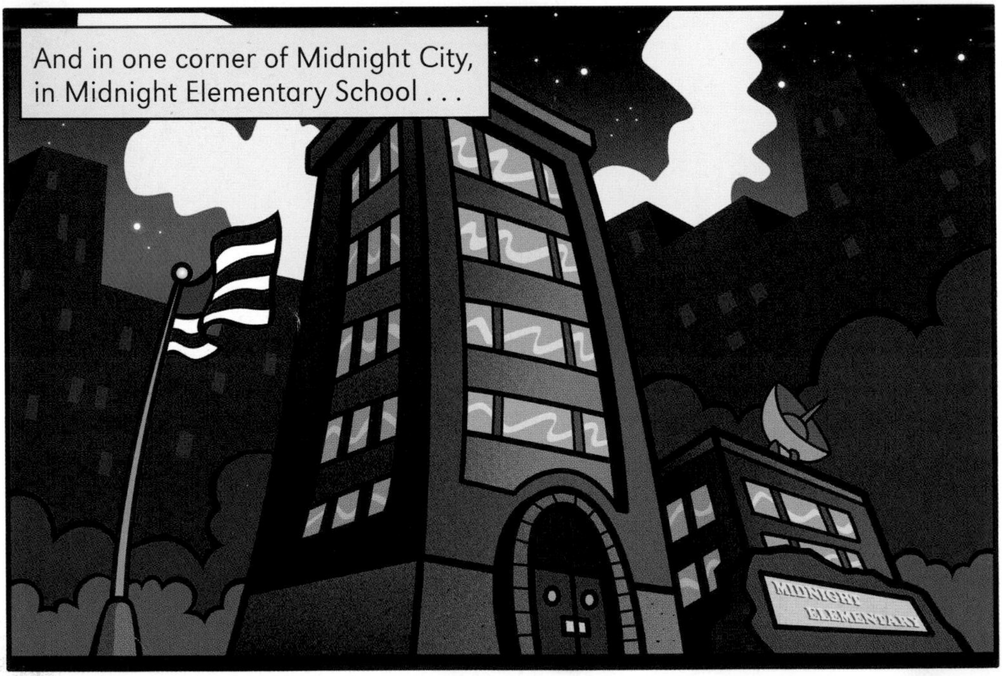
And in one corner of Midnight City, in Midnight Elementary School . . .
MIDNIGHT ELEMENTARY

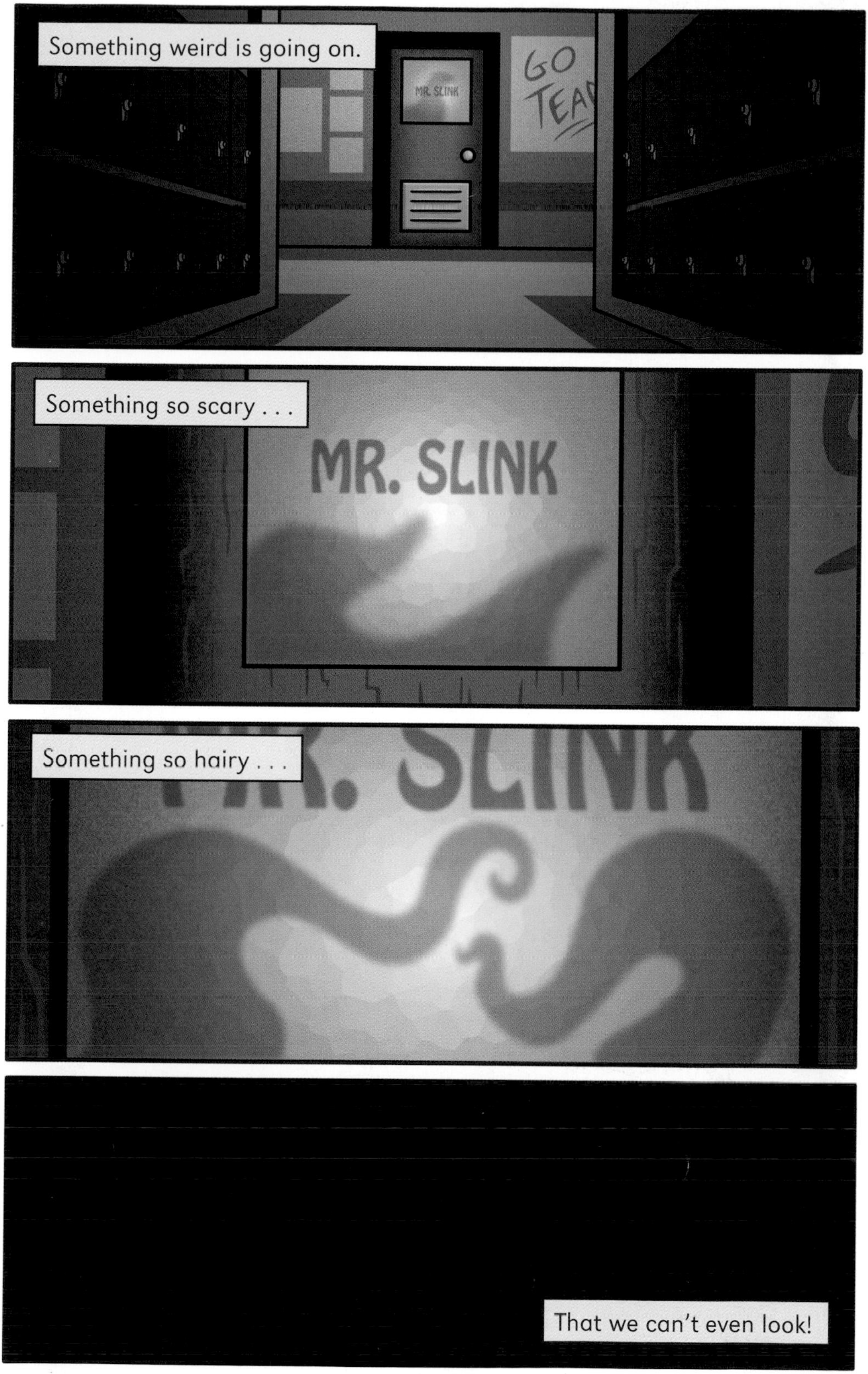
Something weird is going on.
MR. SLINK
Something so scary . . .
MR. SLINK
Something so hairy . . .
That we can't even look!

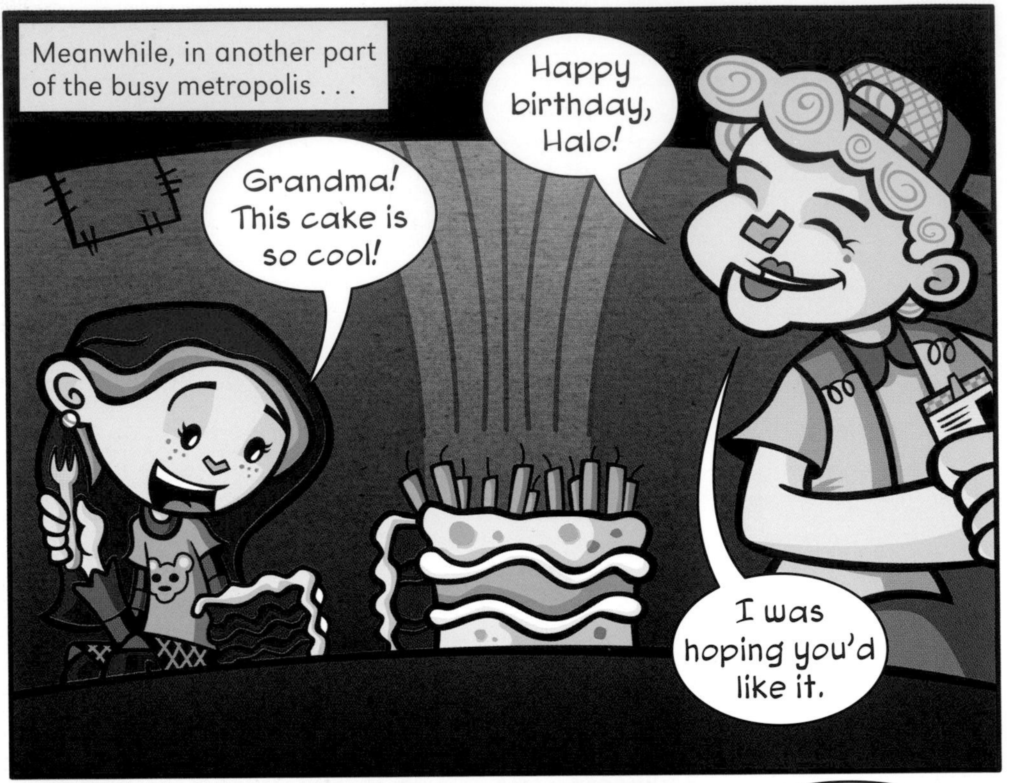
Meanwhile, in another part of the busy metropolis . . .
Happy birthday, Halo!
Grandma! This cake is so cool!
I was hoping you'd like it.

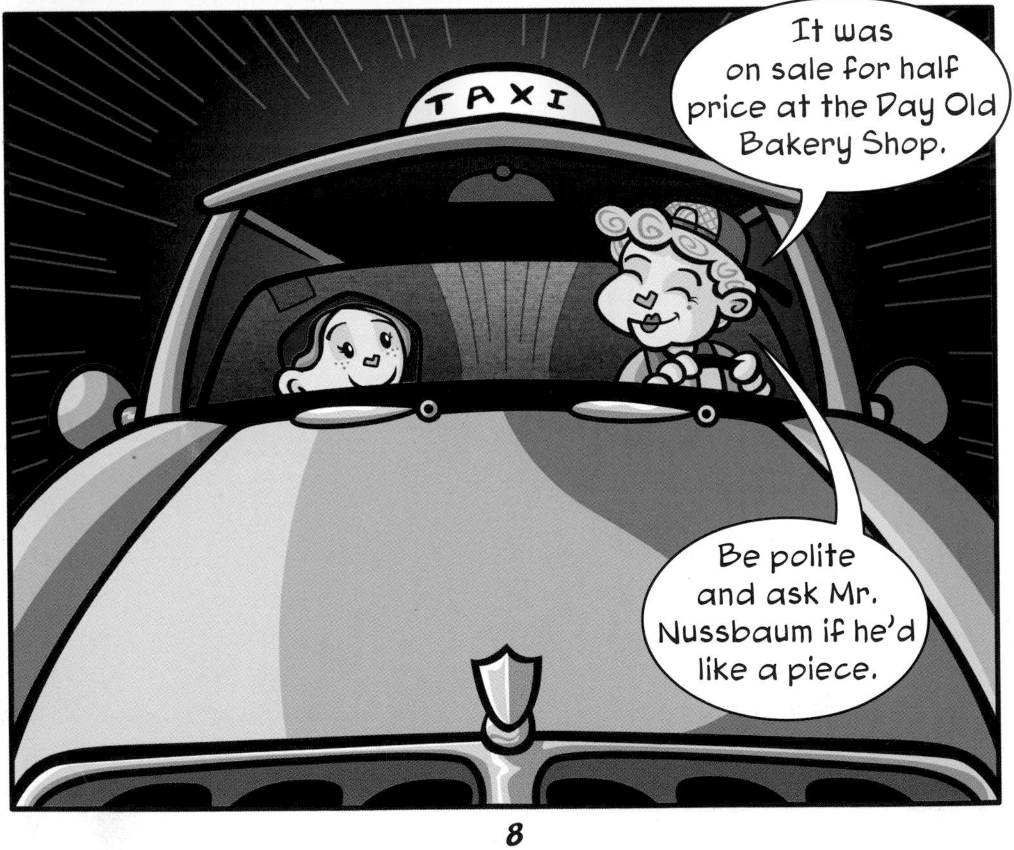
TAXI
It was on sale for half price at the Day Old Bakery Shop.
Be polite and ask Mr. Nussbaum if he'd like a piece.

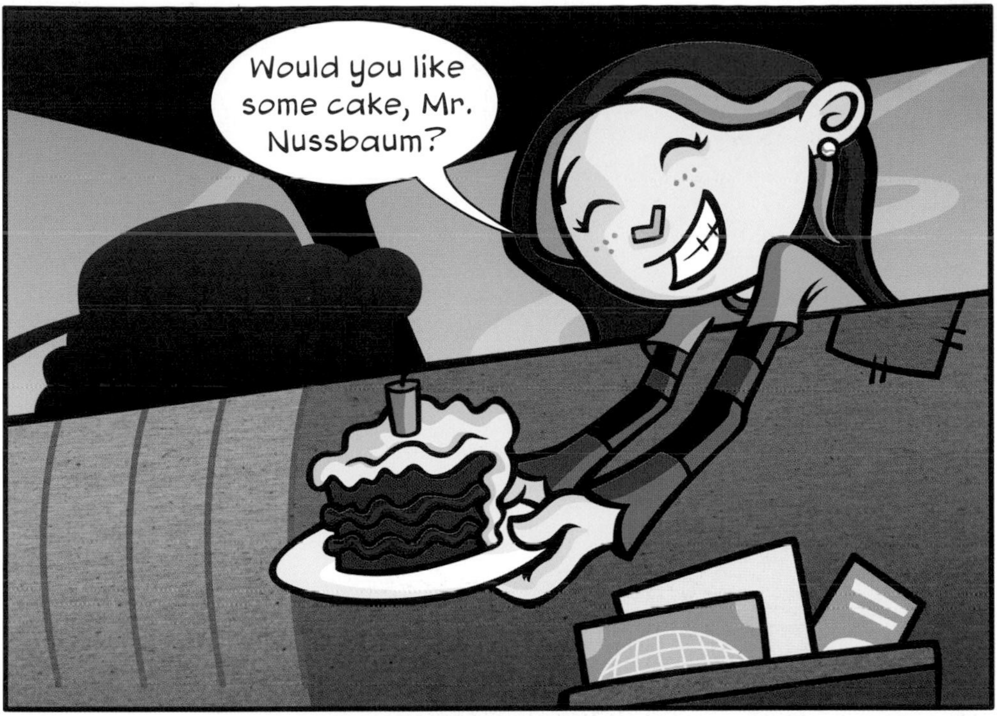
Would you like some cake, Mr. Nussbaum?

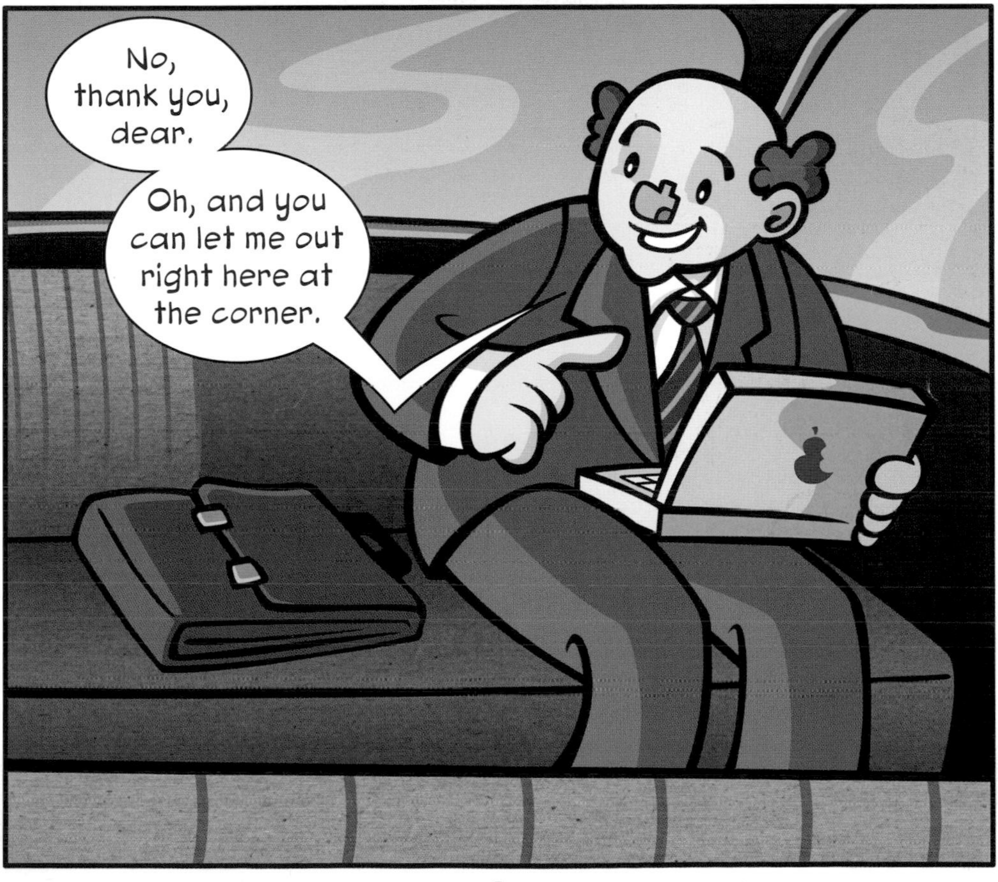
No, thank you, dear.
Oh, and you can let me out right here at the corner.

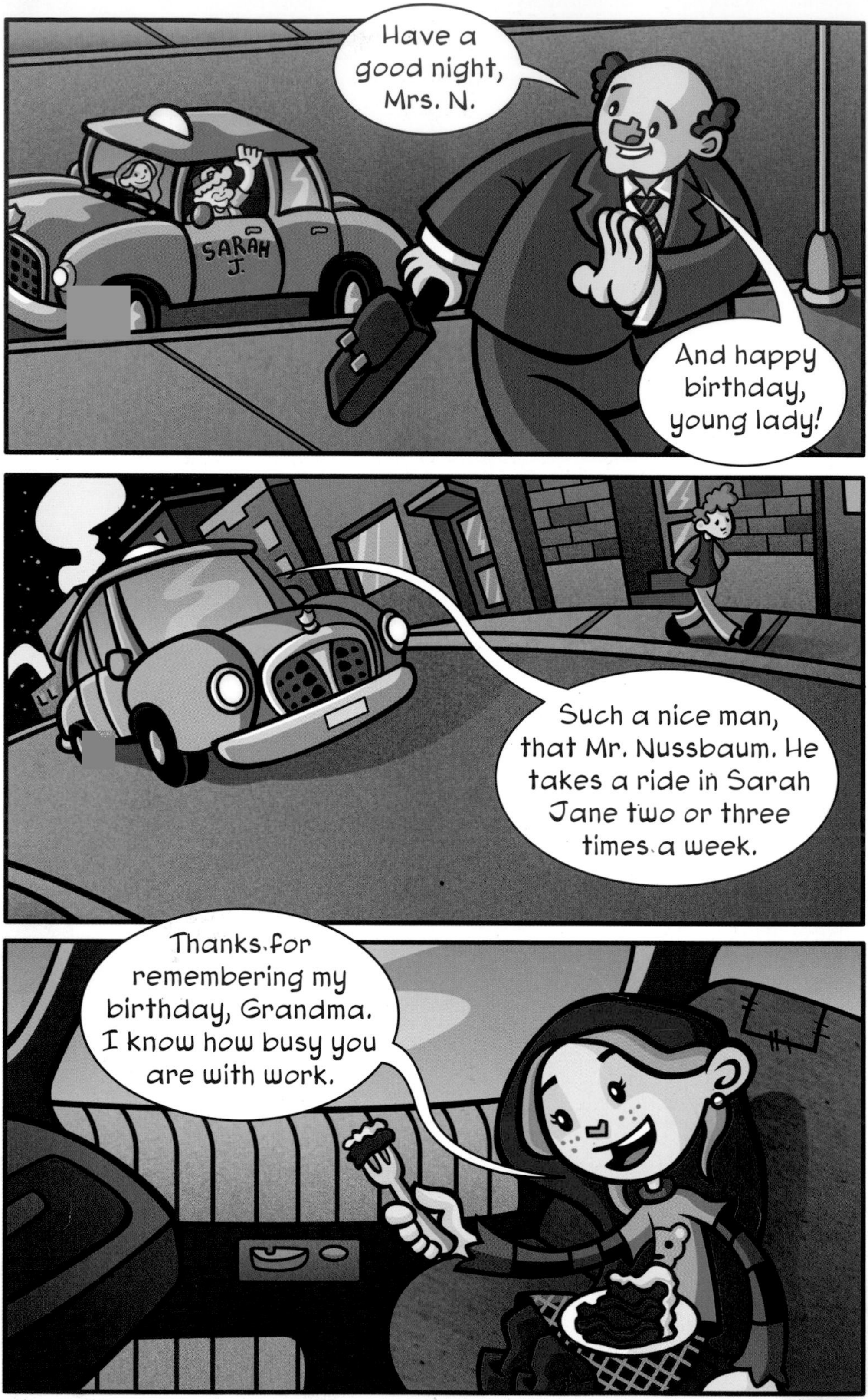
Have a good night, Mrs. N.
SARAH J.
And happy birthday, young lady!
Such a nice man, that Mr. Nussbaum. He takes a ride in Sarah Jane two or three times a week.
Thanks for remembering my birthday, Grandma. I know how busy you are with work.

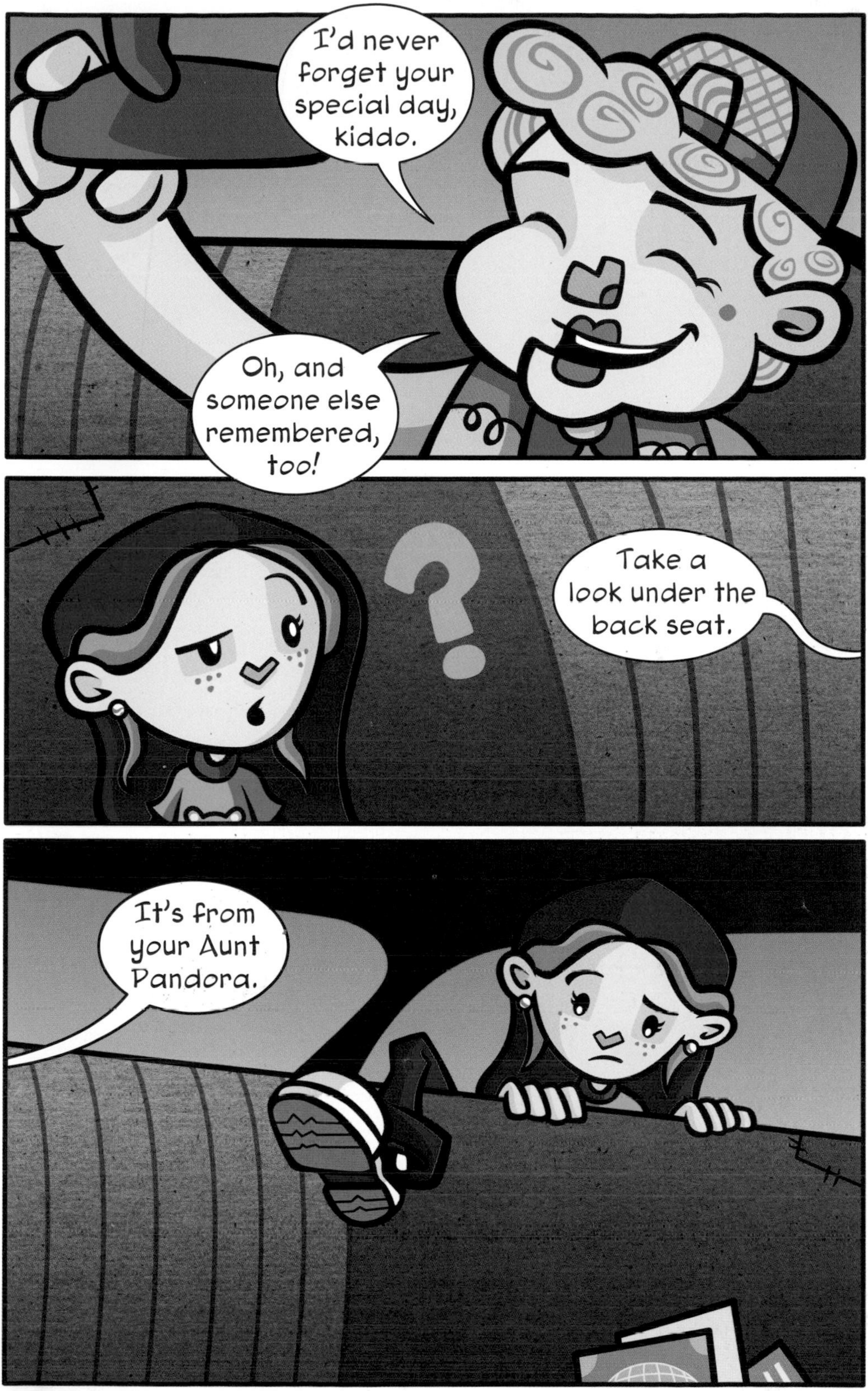

I'd never forget your special day, kiddo.
Oh, and someone else remembered, too!
Take a look under the back seat.
It's from your Aunt Pandora.

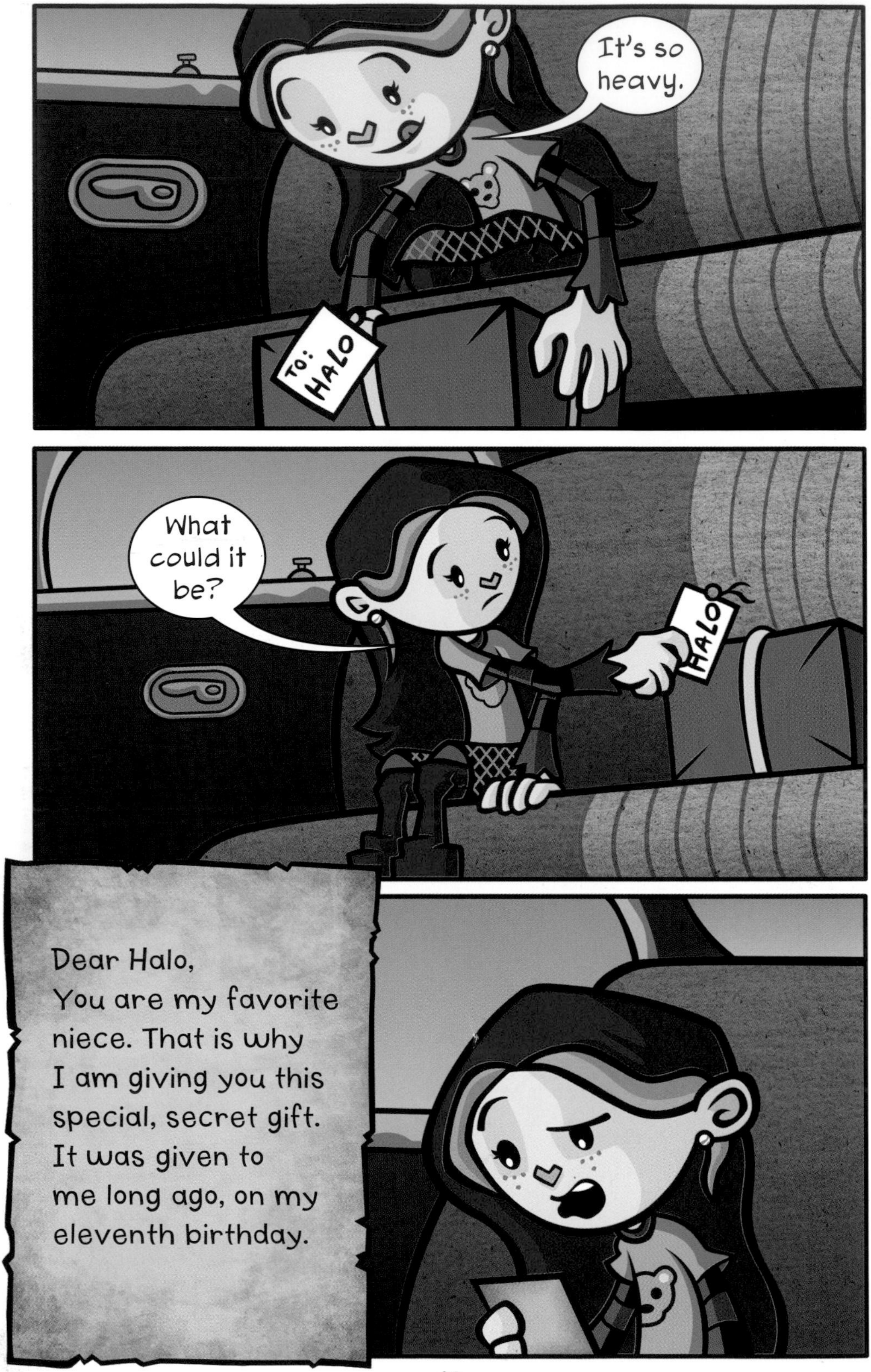
It's so heavy.
TO: HALO
What could it be?
HALO
Dear Halo,
You are my favorite niece. That is why I am giving you this special, secret gift. It was given to me long ago, on my eleventh birthday.

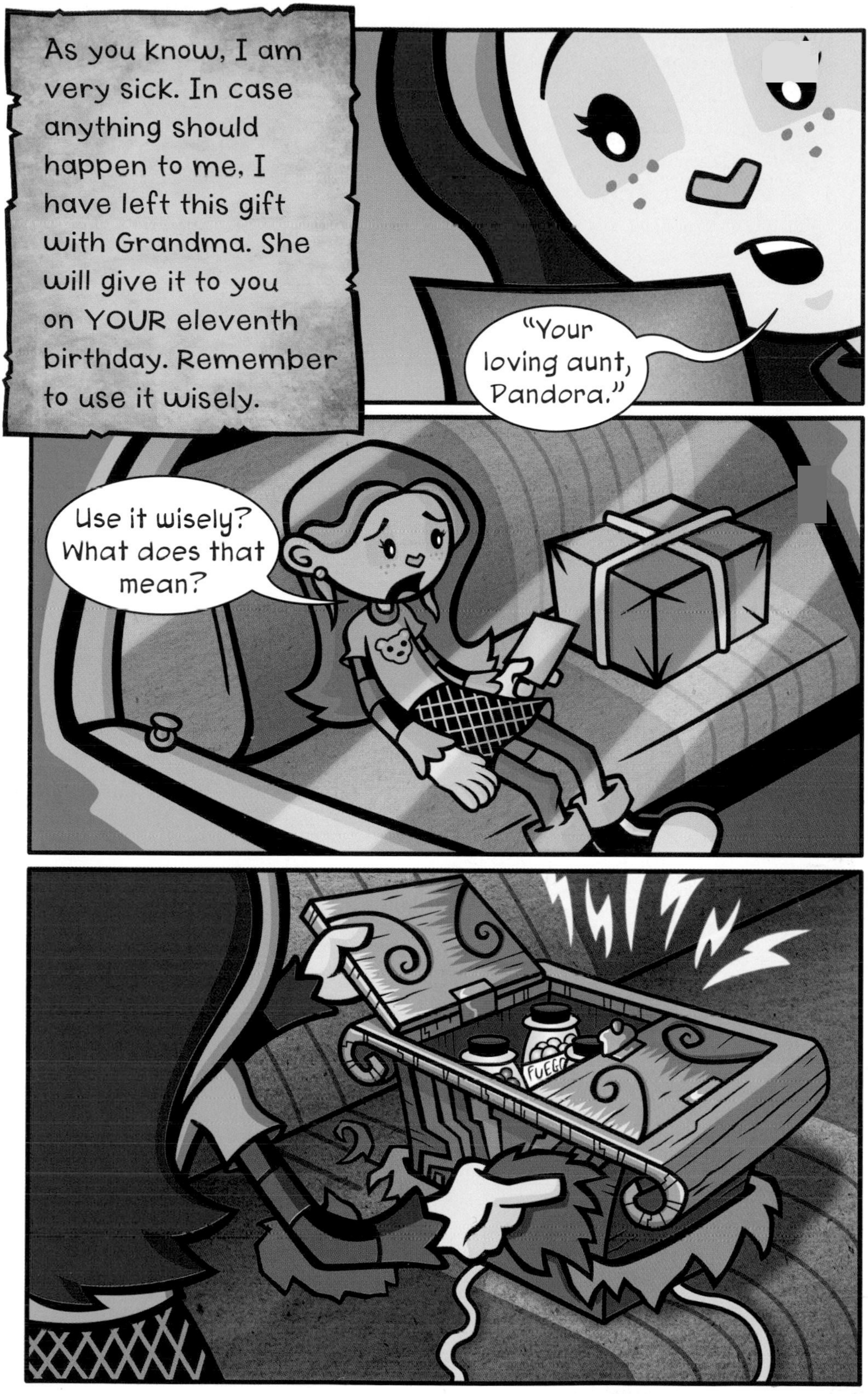

As you know, I am very sick. In case anything should happen to me, I have left this gift with Grandma. She will give it to you on YOUR eleventh birthday. Remember to use it wisely.
"Your loving aunt, Pandora."
Use it wisely? What does that mean?
FUEGO

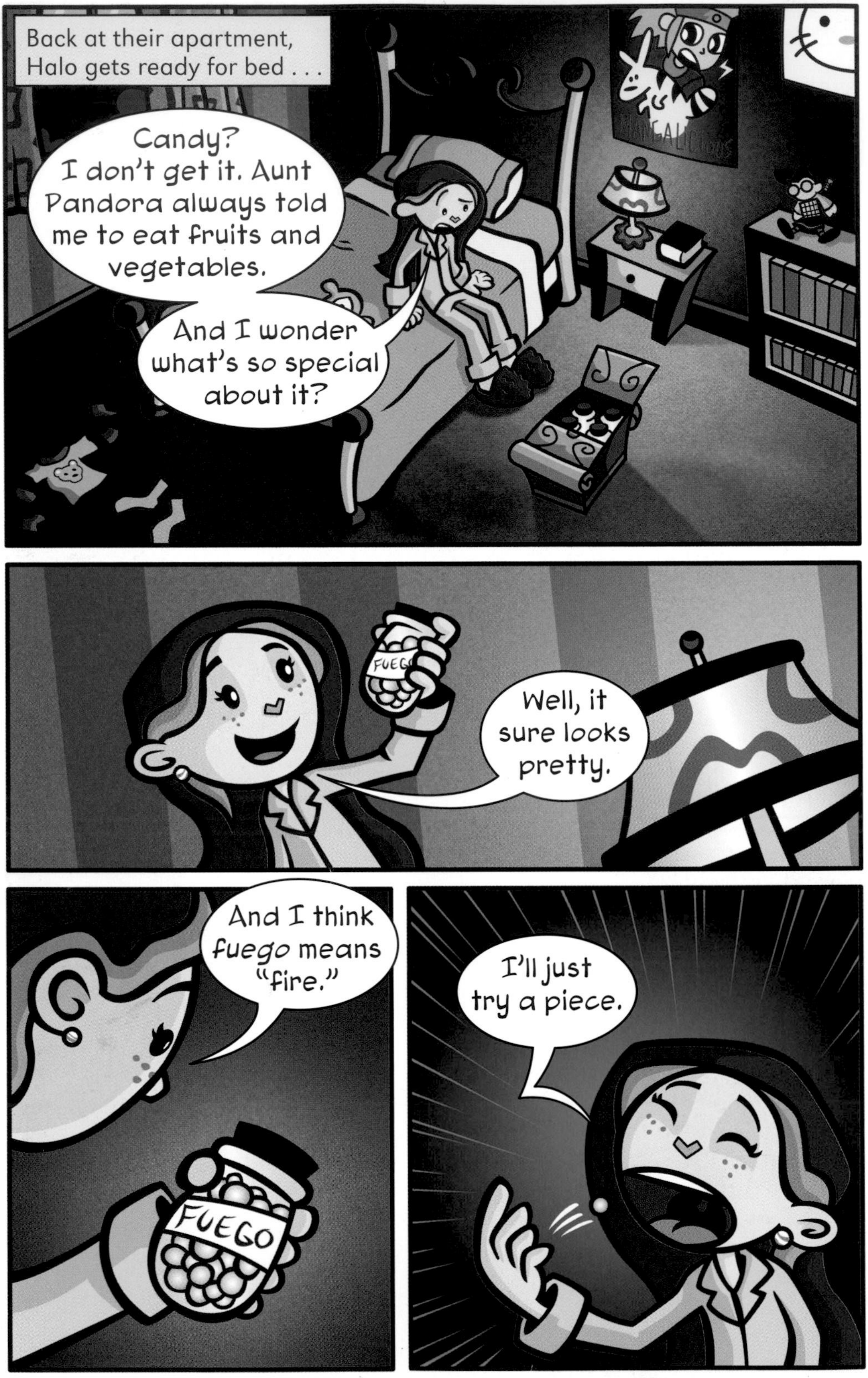
Back at their apartment, Halo gets ready for bed . . .
Candy? I don't get it. Aunt Pandora always told me to eat fruits and vegetables.
And I wonder what's so special about it?
FUEGO
Well, it sure looks pretty.
And I think *fuego* means "fire."
FUEGO
I'll just try a piece.

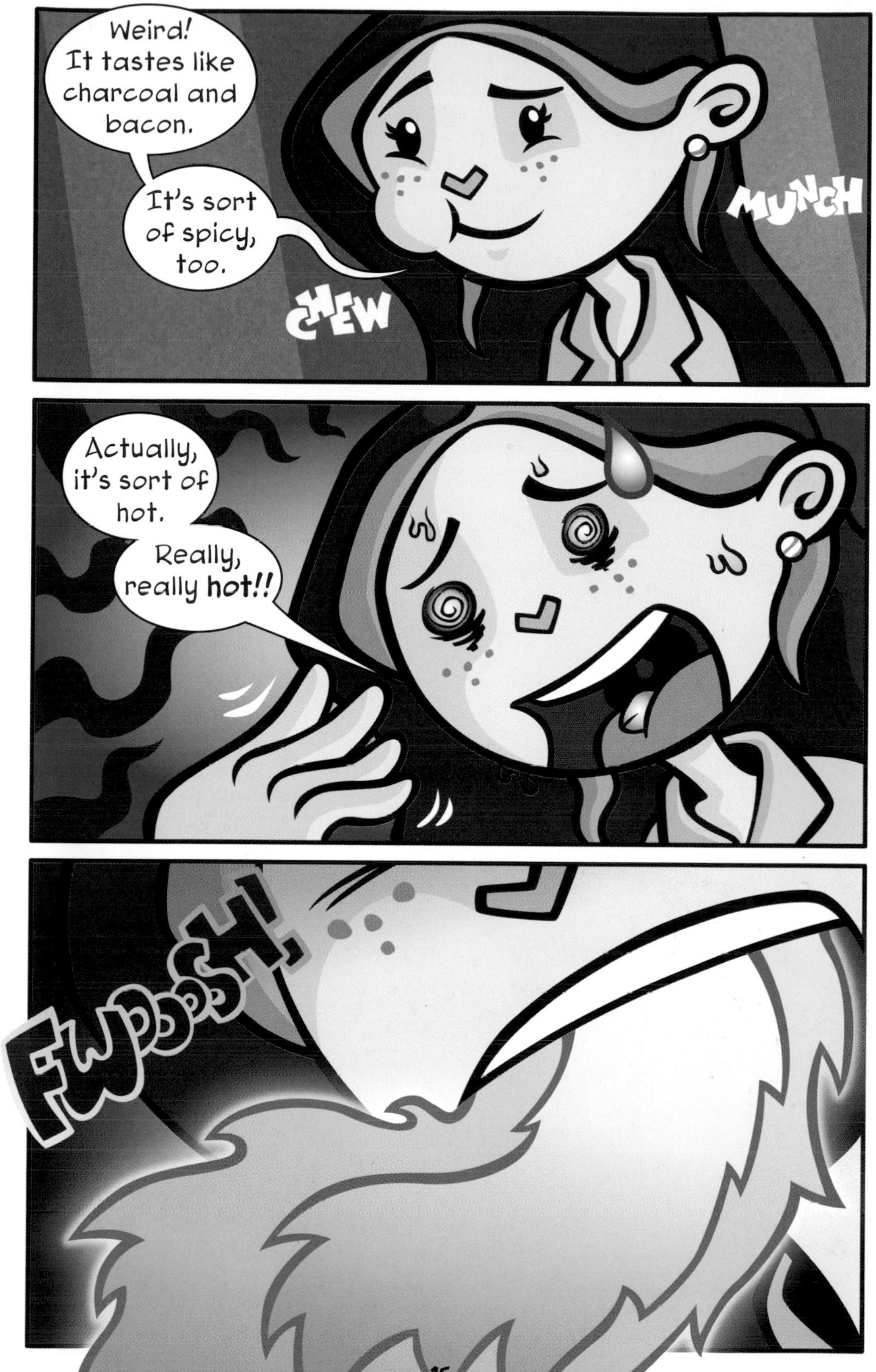
Weird! It tastes like charcoal and bacon.
It's sort of spicy, too.
MUNCH
CHEW
Actually, it's sort of hot.
Really, really **hot**!!
FWOOSH!

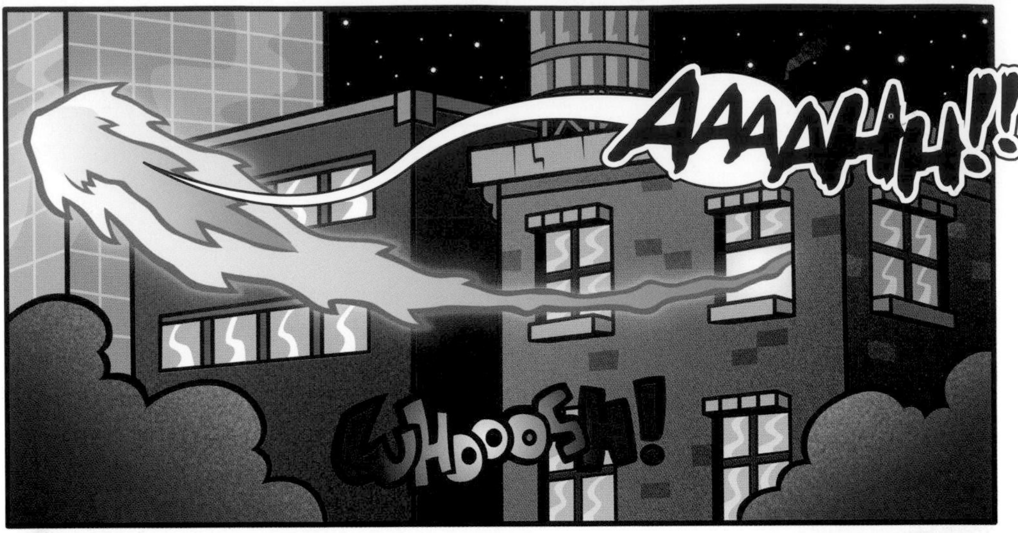
AAAAHHH!?!
WHOOOSH!

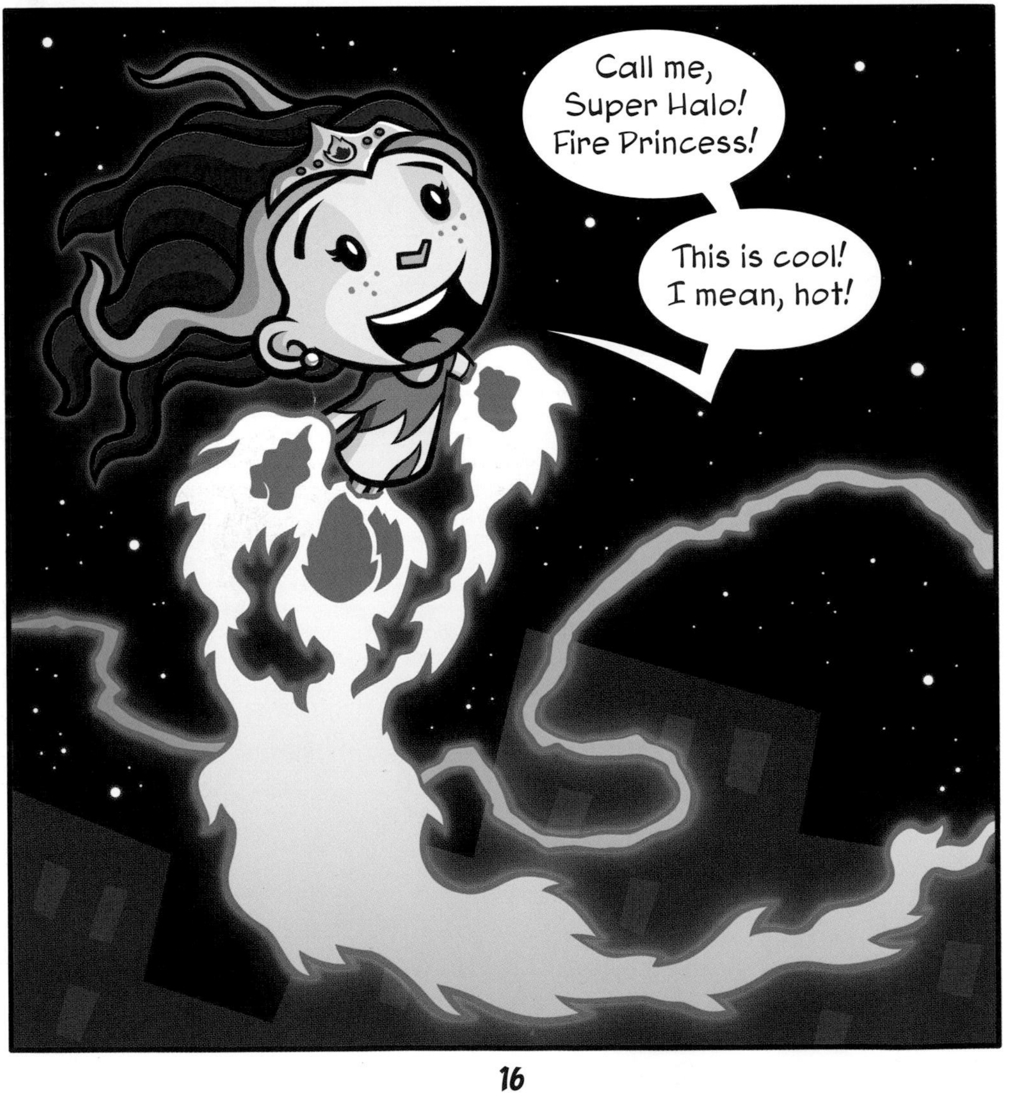
Call me, Super Halo! Fire Princess!
This is cool! I mean, hot!

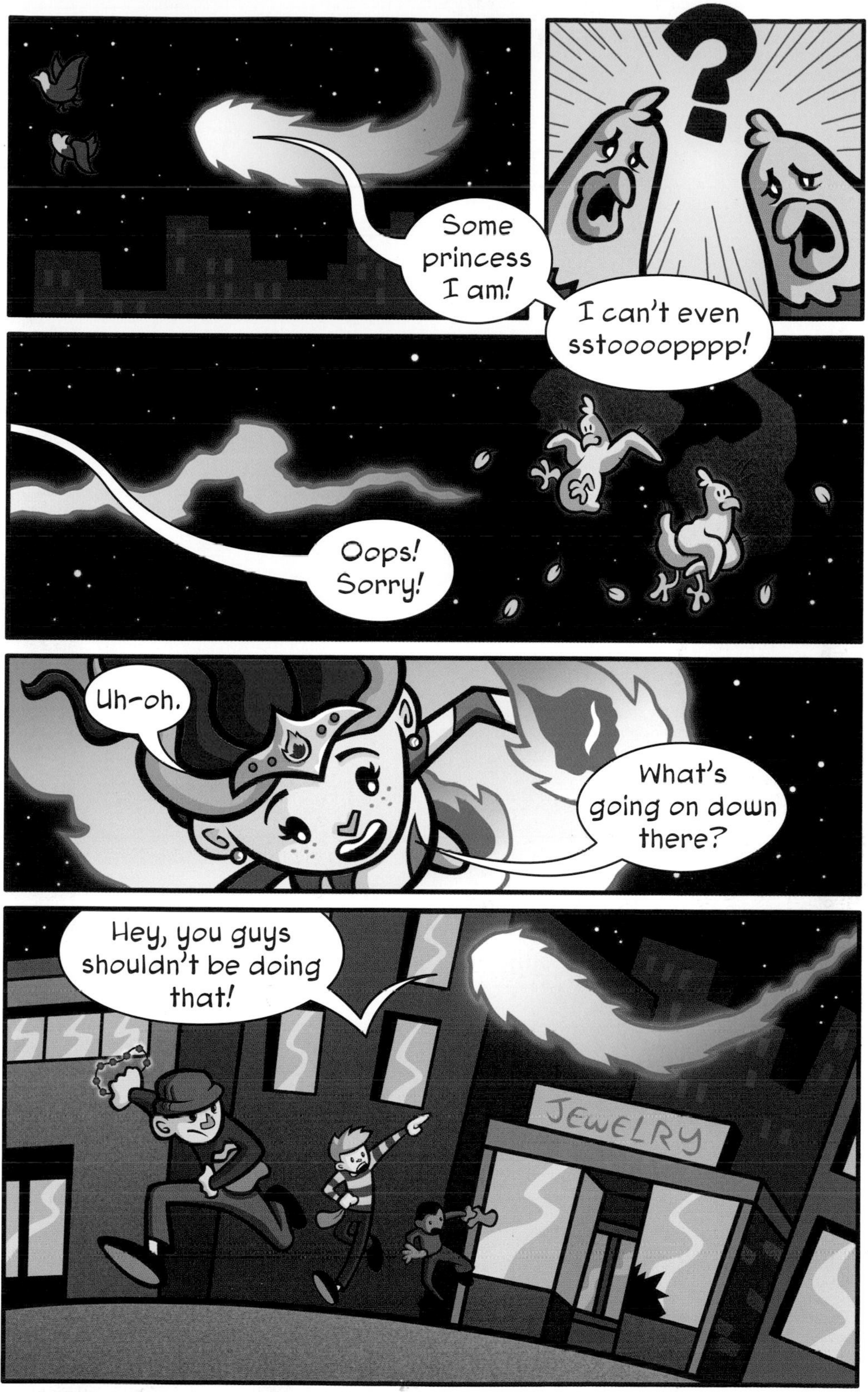

Some princess I am!
I can't even sstoooopppp!
Oops! Sorry!
Uh-oh.
What's going on down there?
Hey, you guys shouldn't be doing that!
JEWELRY

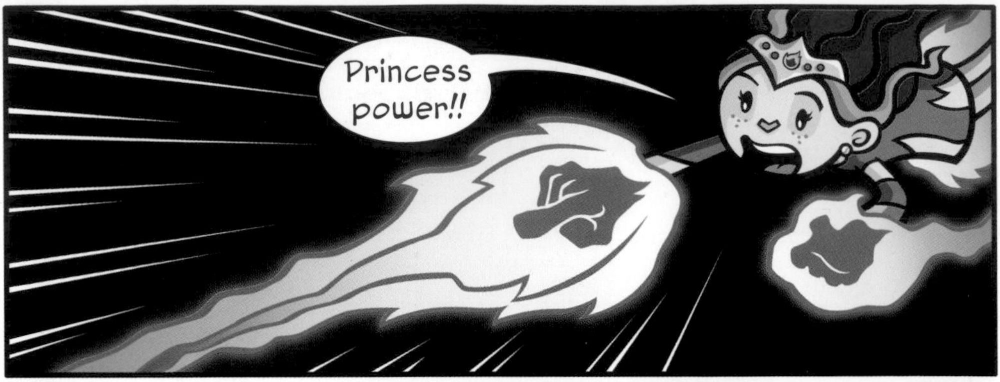
Princess power!!

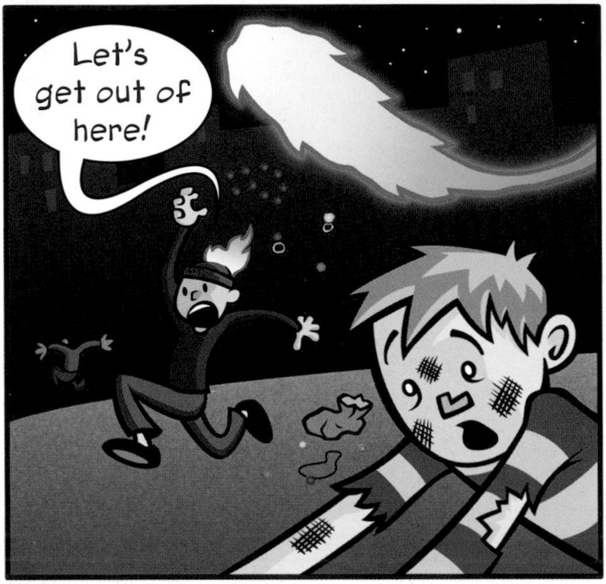
Let's get out of here!

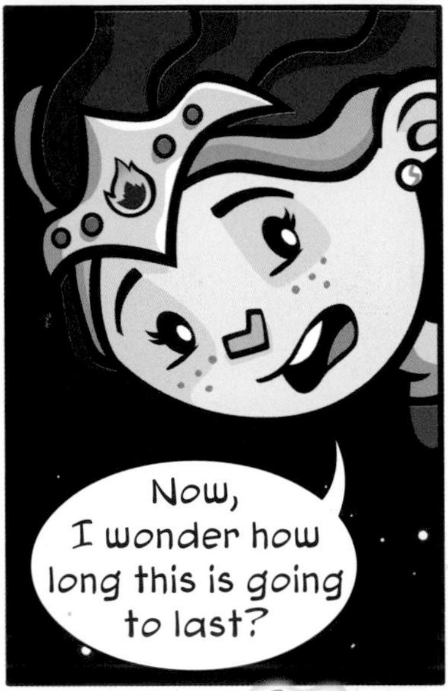
Now, I wonder how long this is going to last?

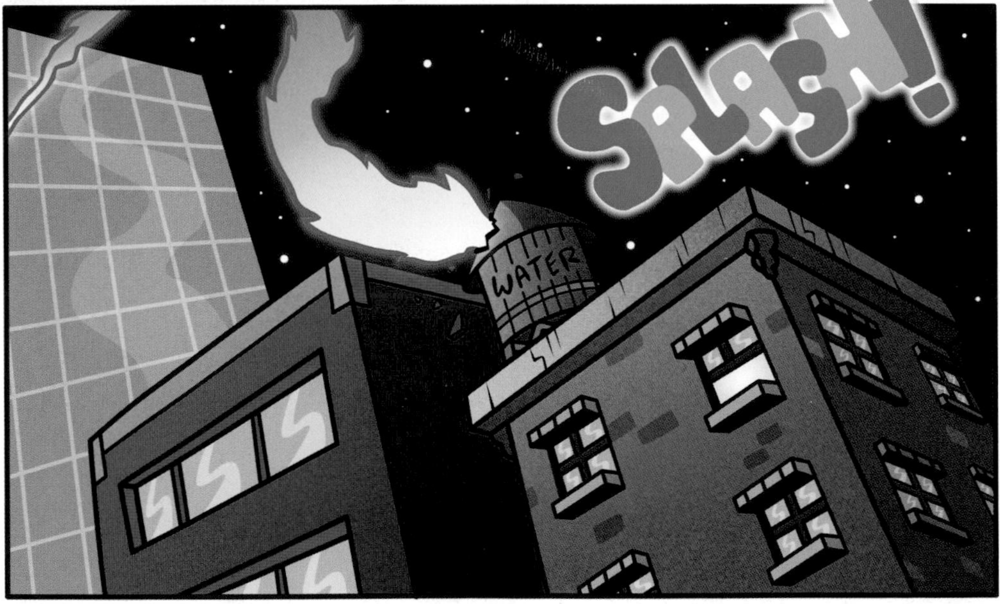
SPLASH!
WATER

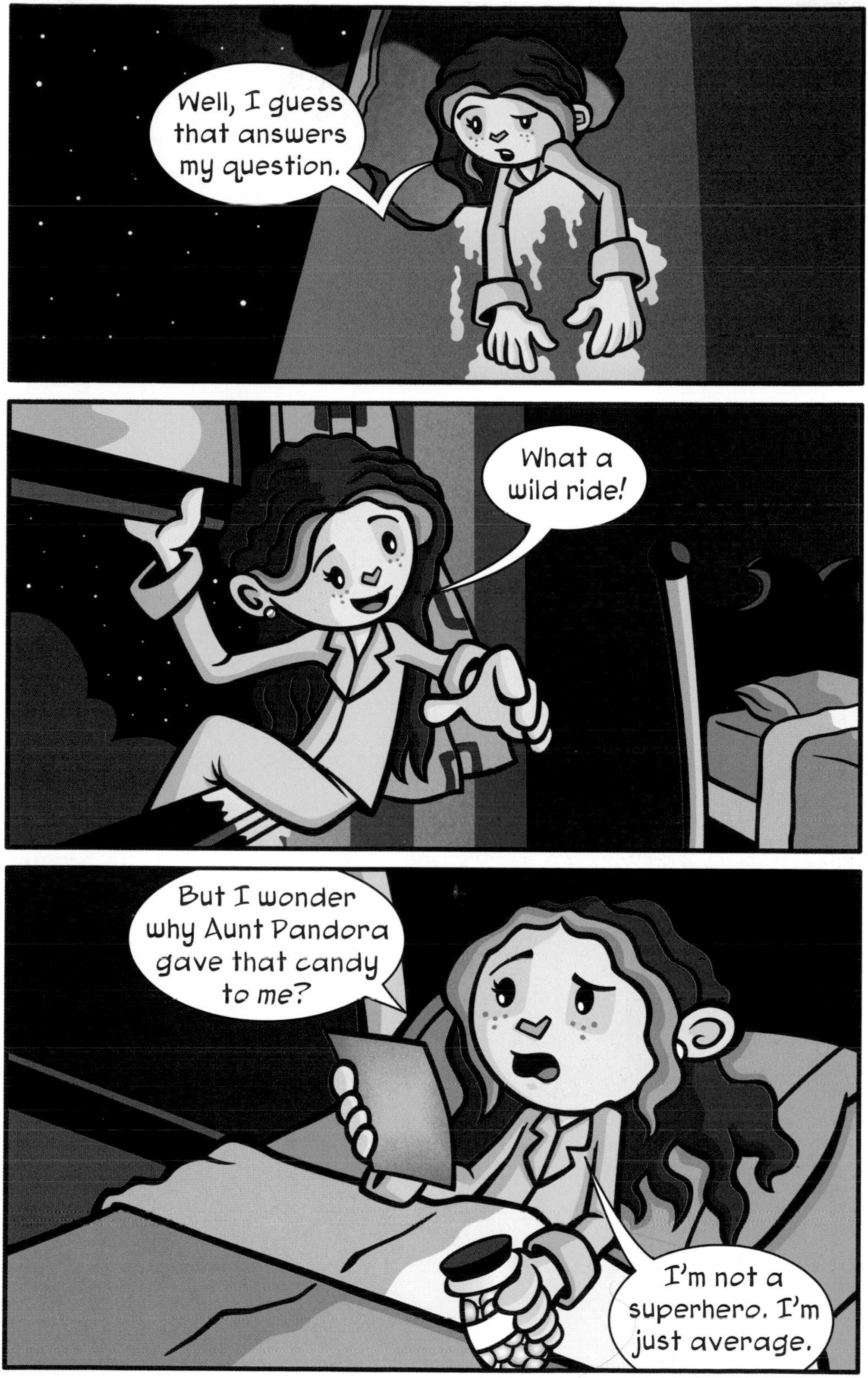
Well, I guess that answers my question.
What a wild ride!
But I wonder why Aunt Pandora gave that candy to me?
I'm not a superhero. I'm just average.

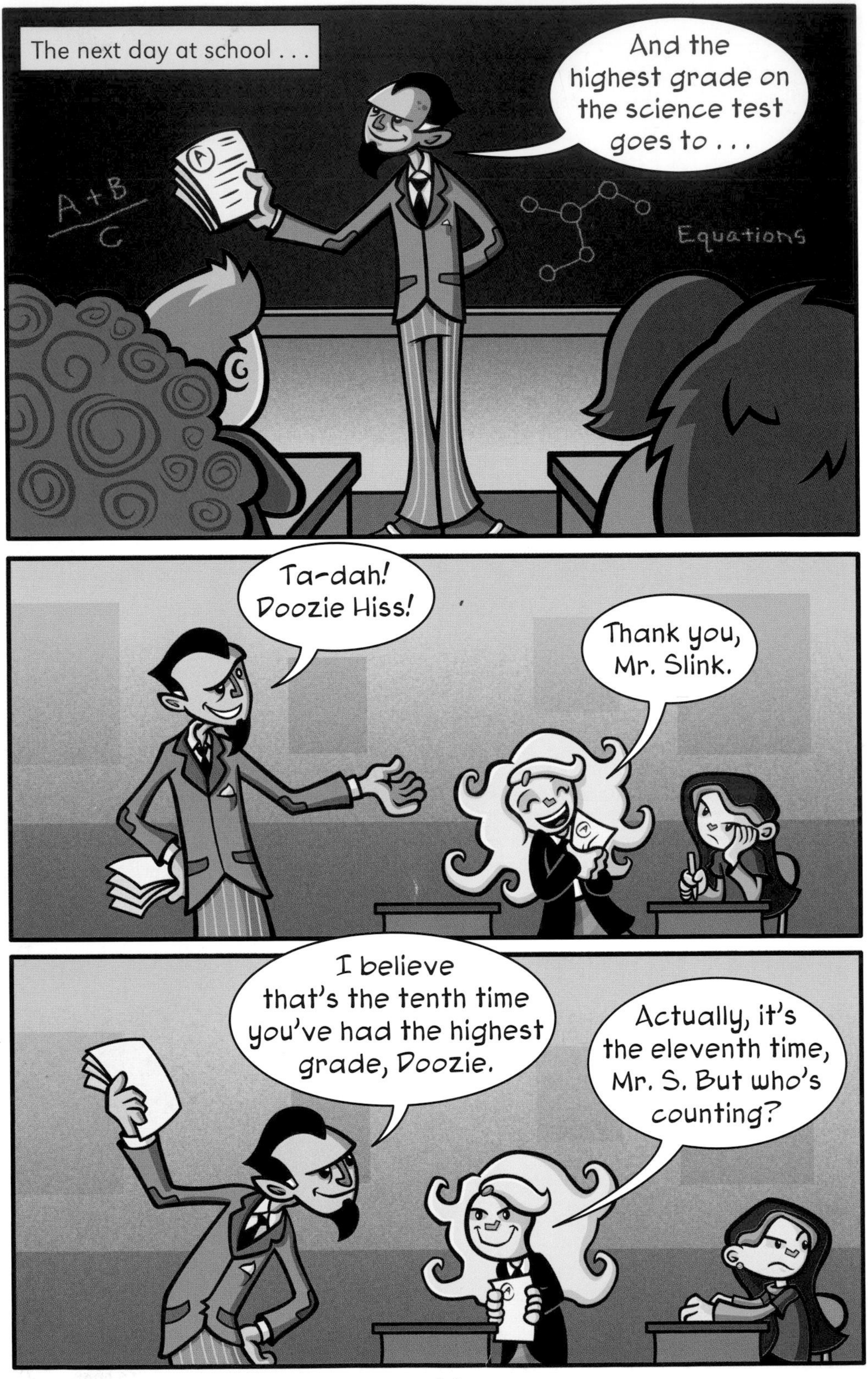
The next day at school . . .
And the highest grade on the science test goes to . . .
A+B / C
Equations
Ta-dah! Doozie Hiss!
Thank you, Mr. Slink.
I believe that's the tenth time you've had the highest grade, Doozie.
Actually, it's the eleventh time, Mr. S. But who's counting?

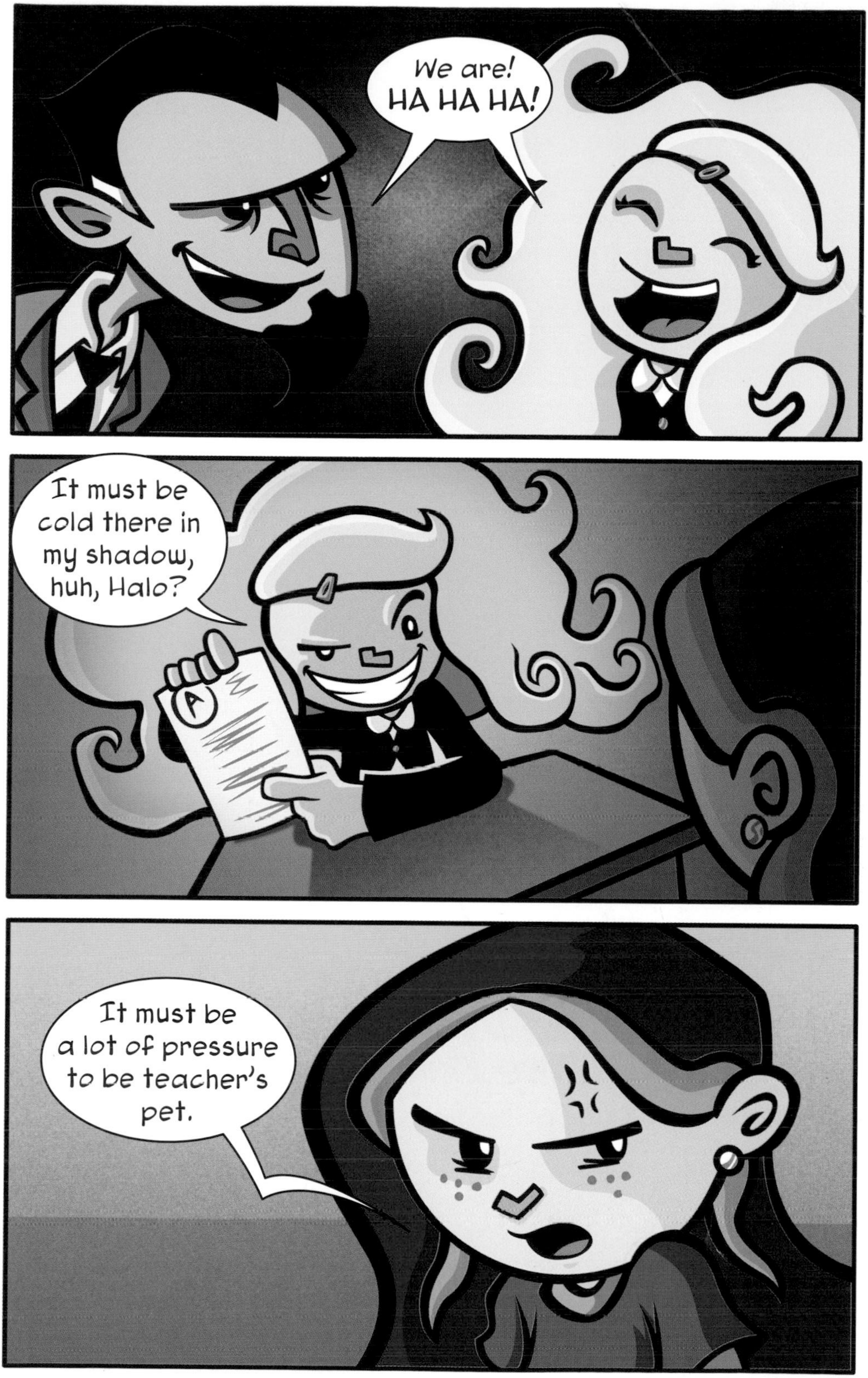
We are! HA HA HA!
It must be cold there in my shadow, huh, Halo?
It must be a lot of pressure to be teacher's pet.

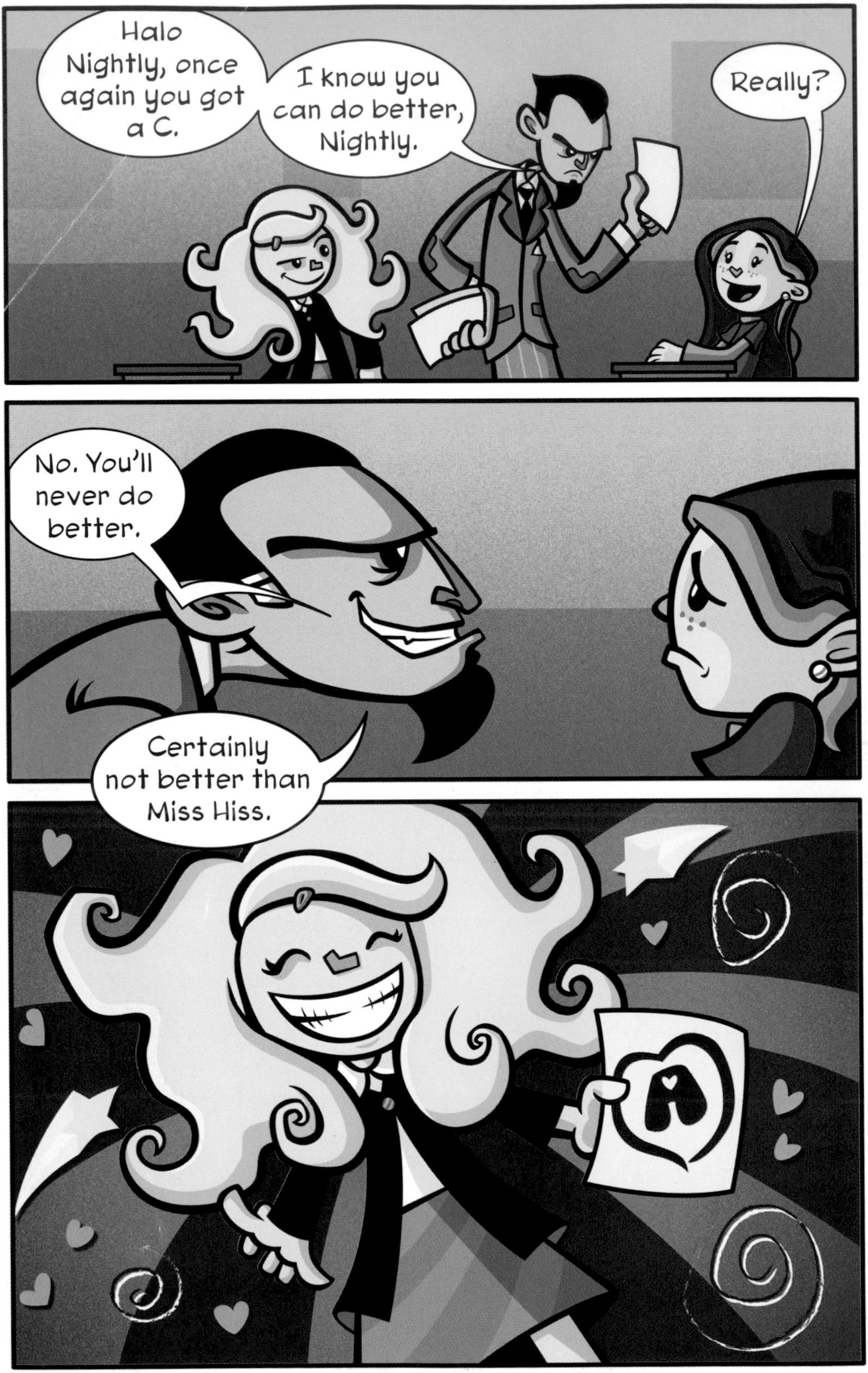
Halo Nightly, once again you got a C.
I know you can do better, Nightly.
Really?
No. You'll never do better.
Certainly not better than Miss Hiss.
A

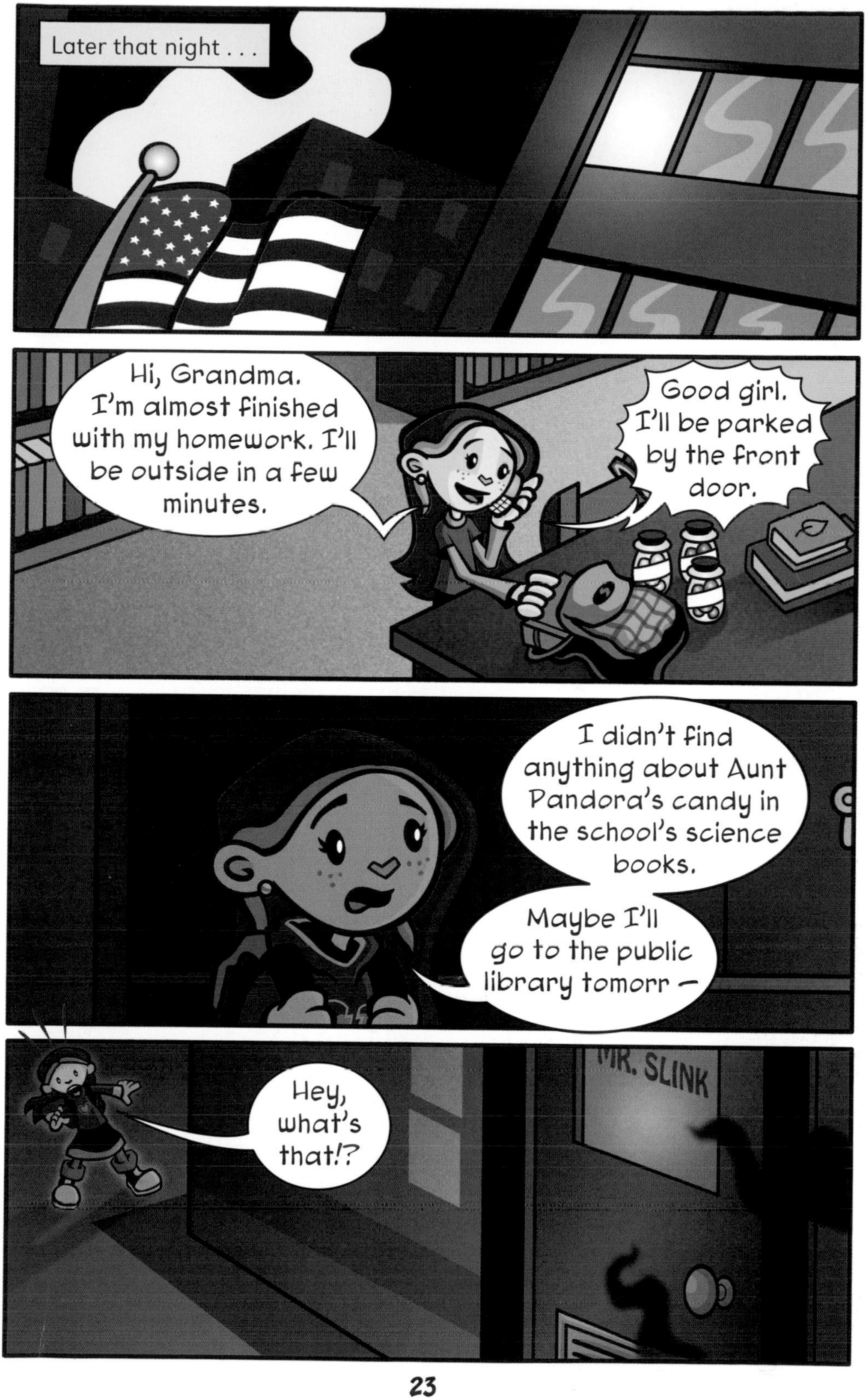
Later that night . . .
Hi, Grandma. I'm almost finished with my homework. I'll be outside in a few minutes.
Good girl. I'll be parked by the front door.
I didn't find anything about Aunt Pandora's candy in the school's science books.
Maybe I'll go to the public library tomorr —
Hey, what's that!?
MR. SLINK

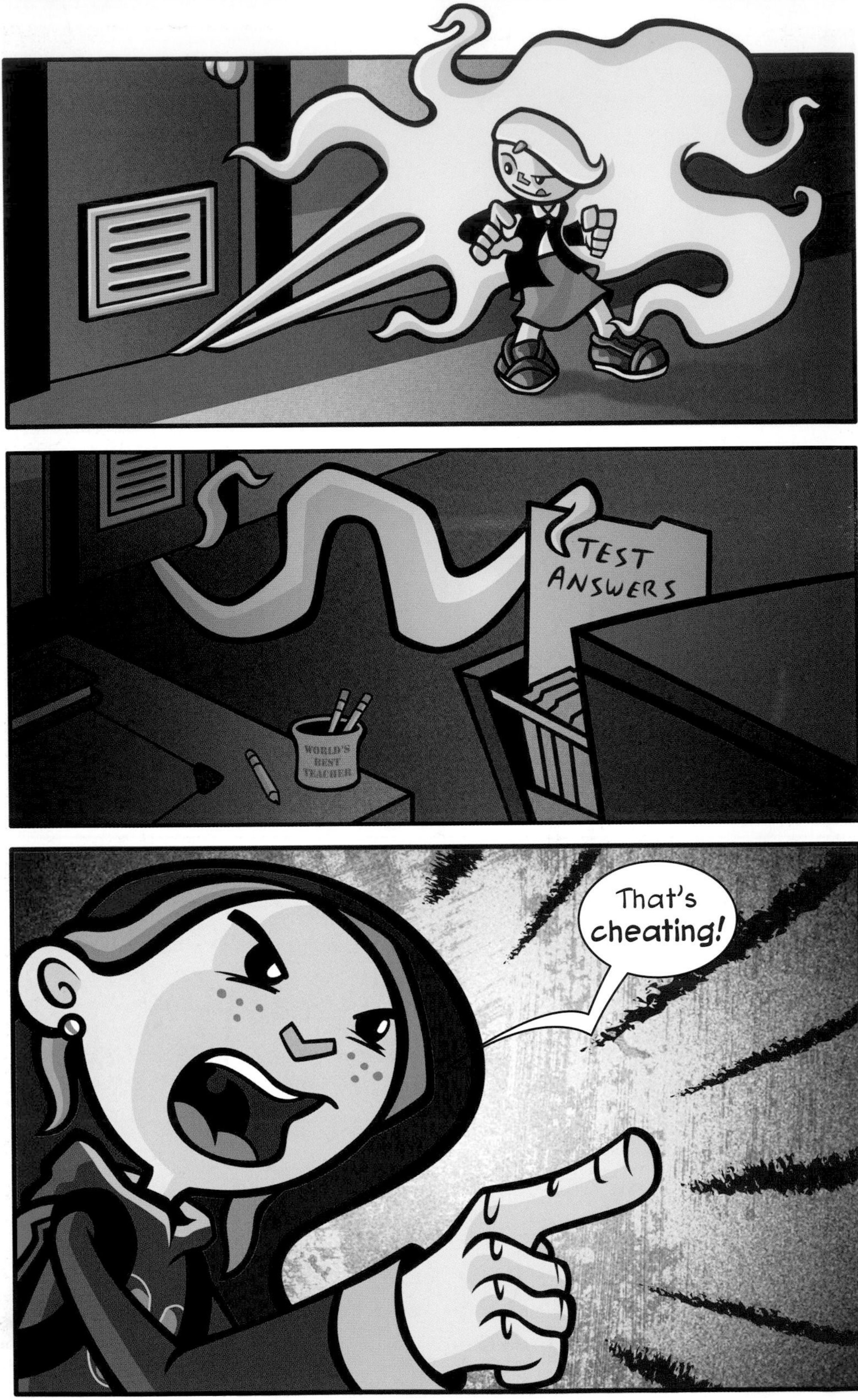
TEST ANSWERS
WORLD'S BEST TEACHER
That's cheating!

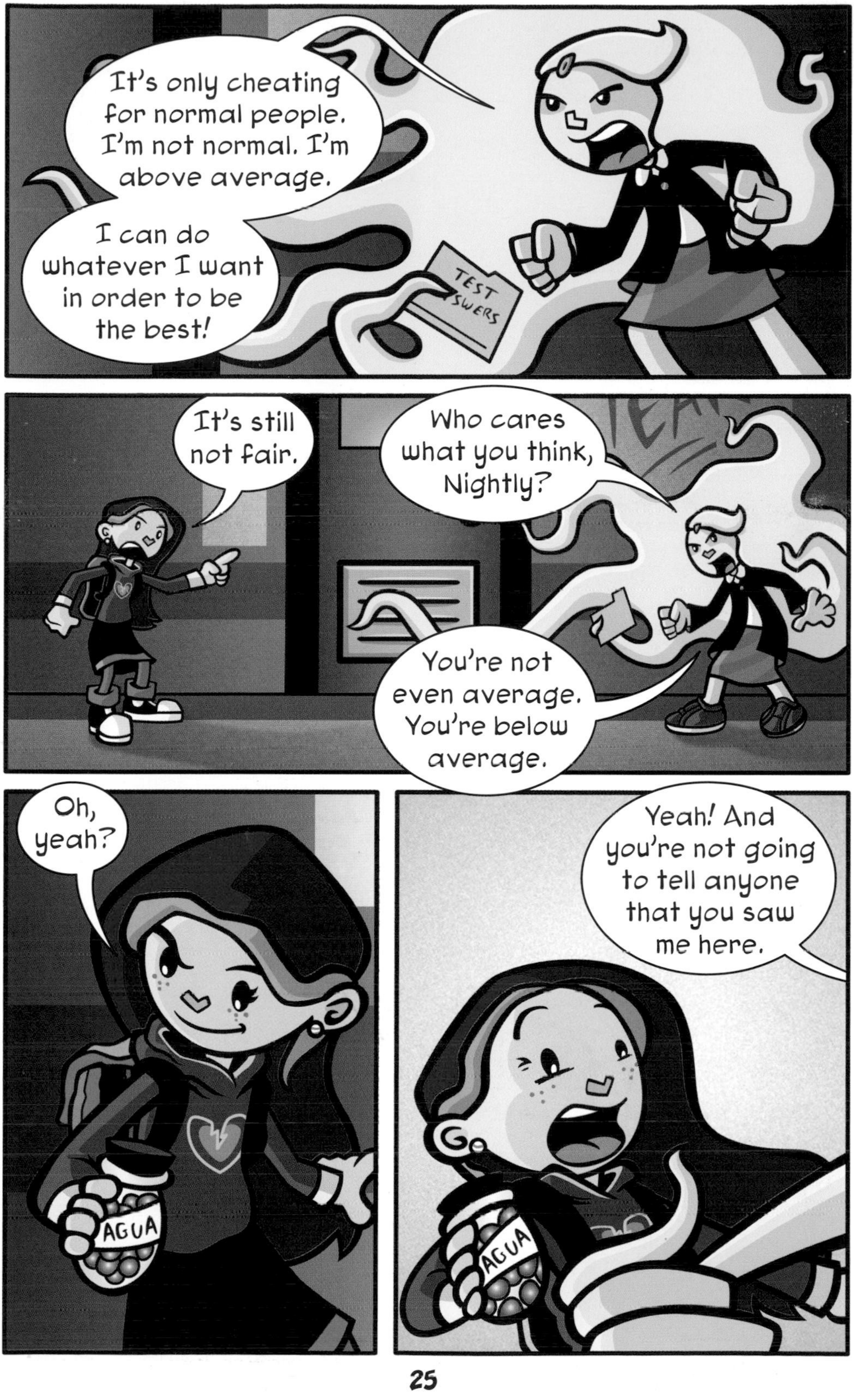
It's only cheating for normal people. I'm not normal. I'm above average.
I can do whatever I want in order to be the best!
TEST SWERS
It's still not fair.
Who cares what you think, Nightly?
You're not even average. You're below average.
Oh, yeah?
AGUA
Yeah! And you're not going to tell anyone that you saw me here.
AGUA

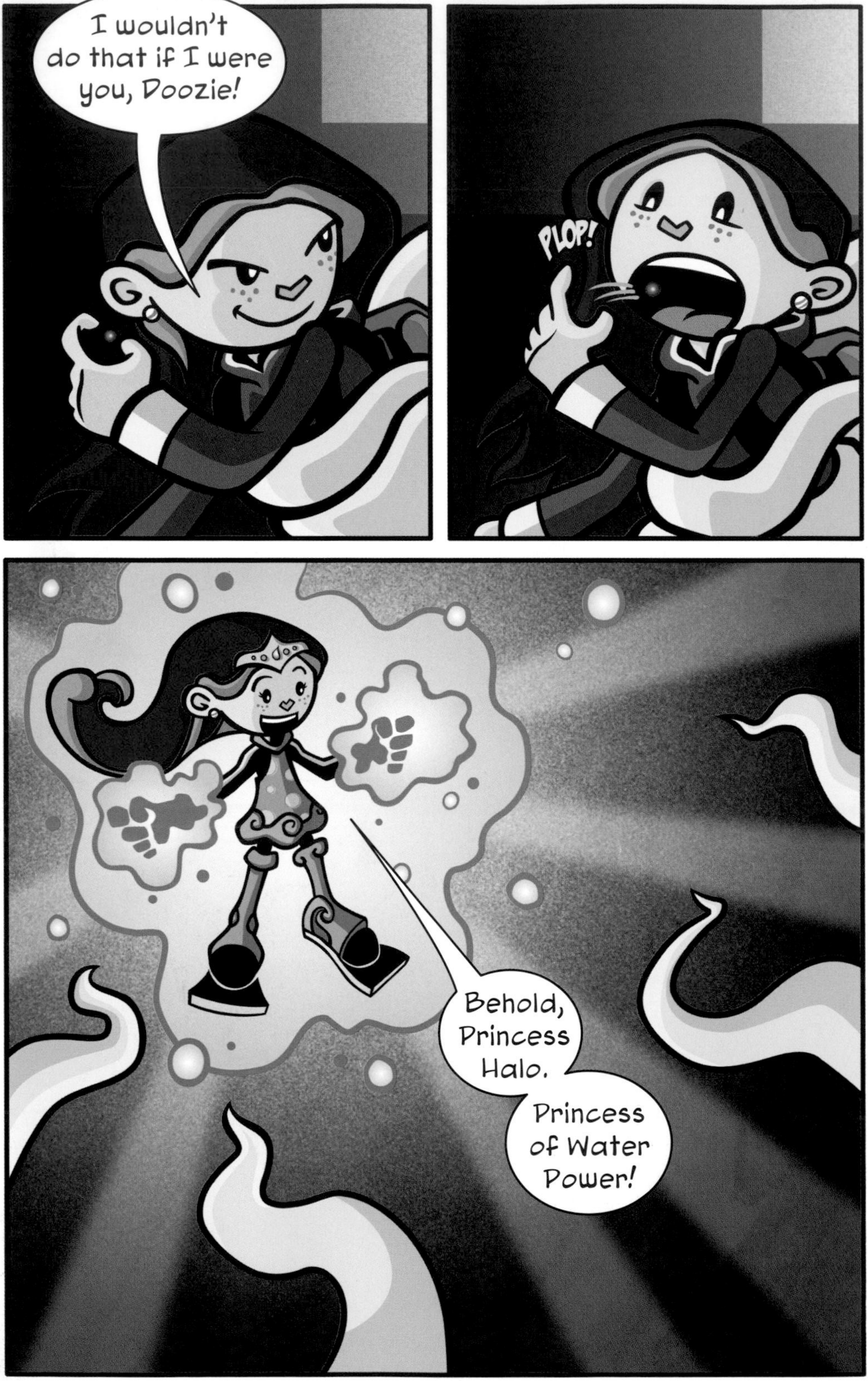
I wouldn't do that if I were you, Doozie!
PLOP!
Behold, Princess Halo.
Princess of Water Power!

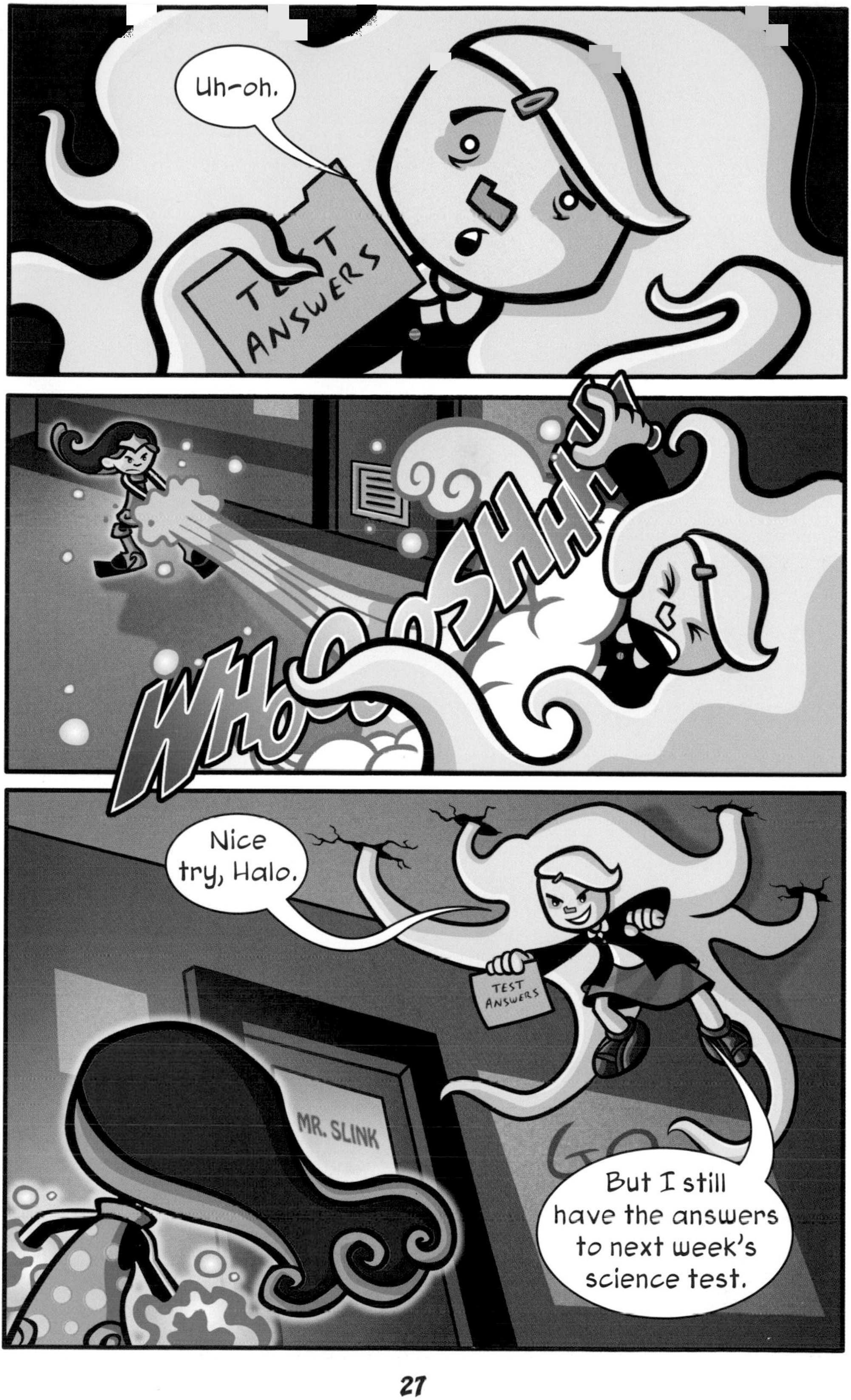
Uh-oh.
TEST ANSWERS
WHOOOOSHHH!
Nice try, Halo.
TEST ANSWERS
MR. SLINK
But I still have the answers to next week's science test.

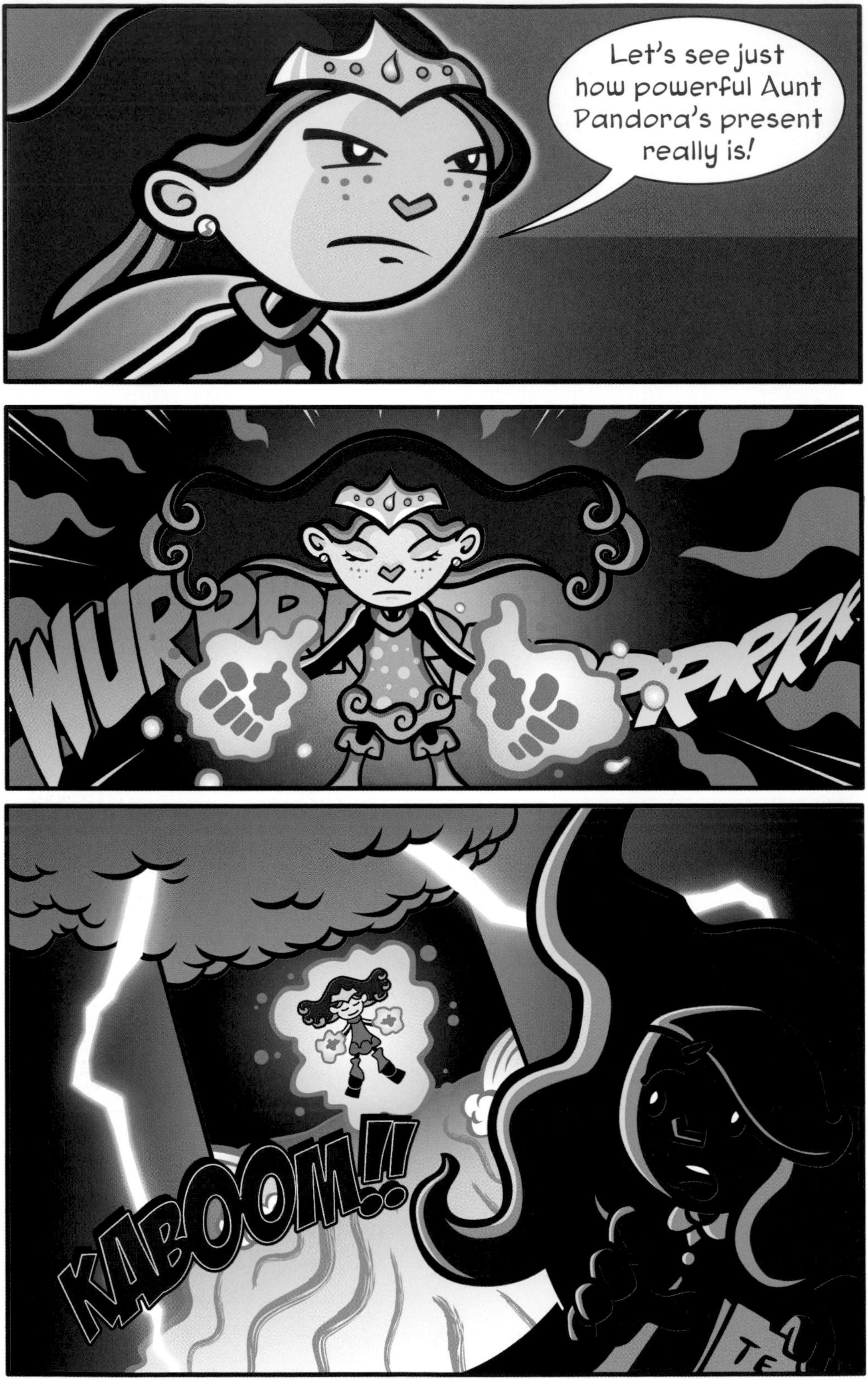
Let's see just how powerful Aunt Pandora's present really is!
KABOOM!!

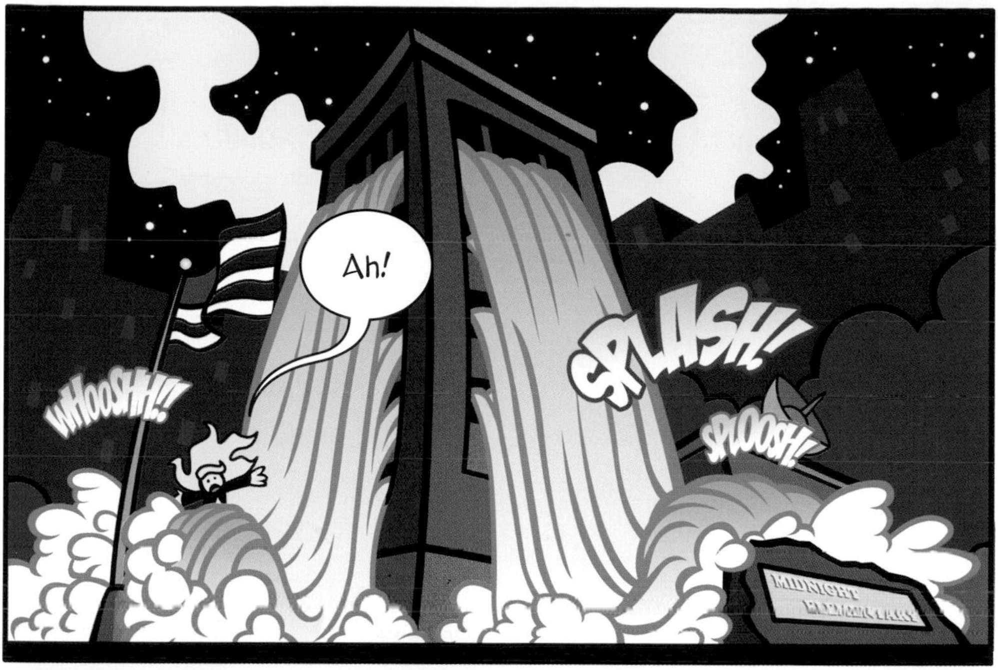
Ah!
WHOOSHH!!
SPLASH!
SPLOOSH!
MIDNIGHT

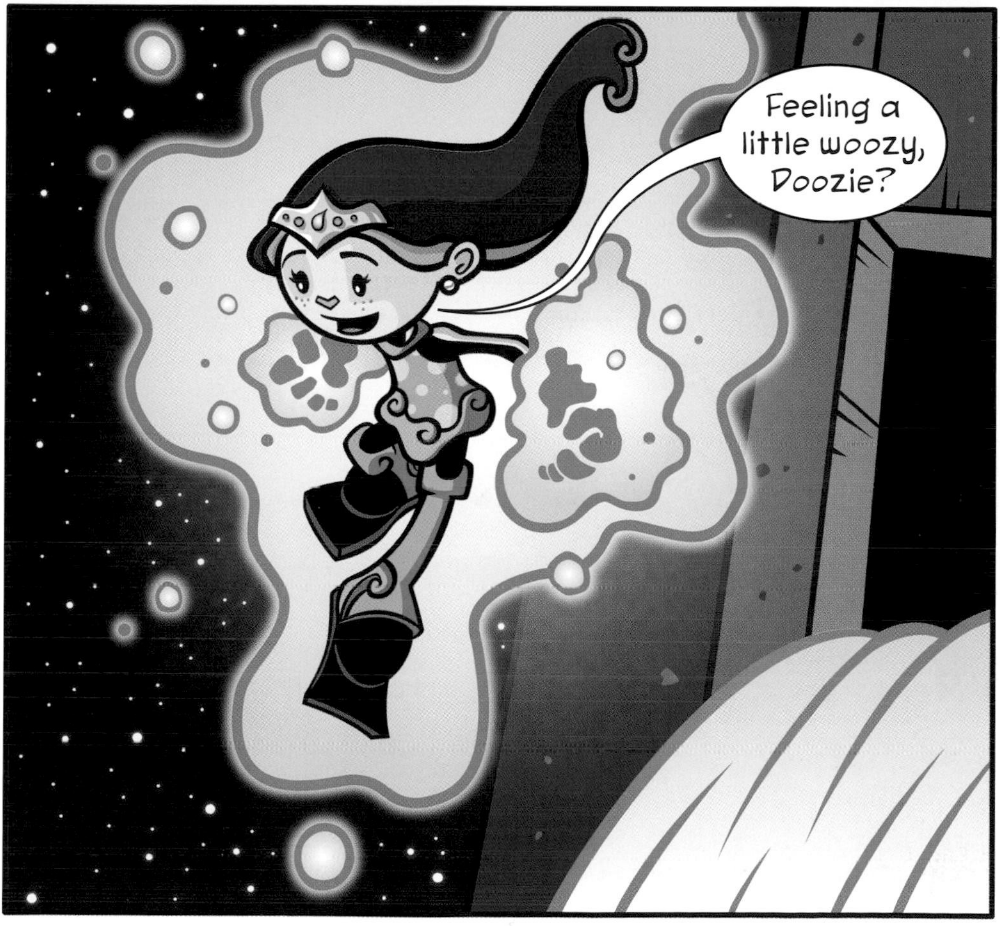
Feeling a little woozy, Doozie?

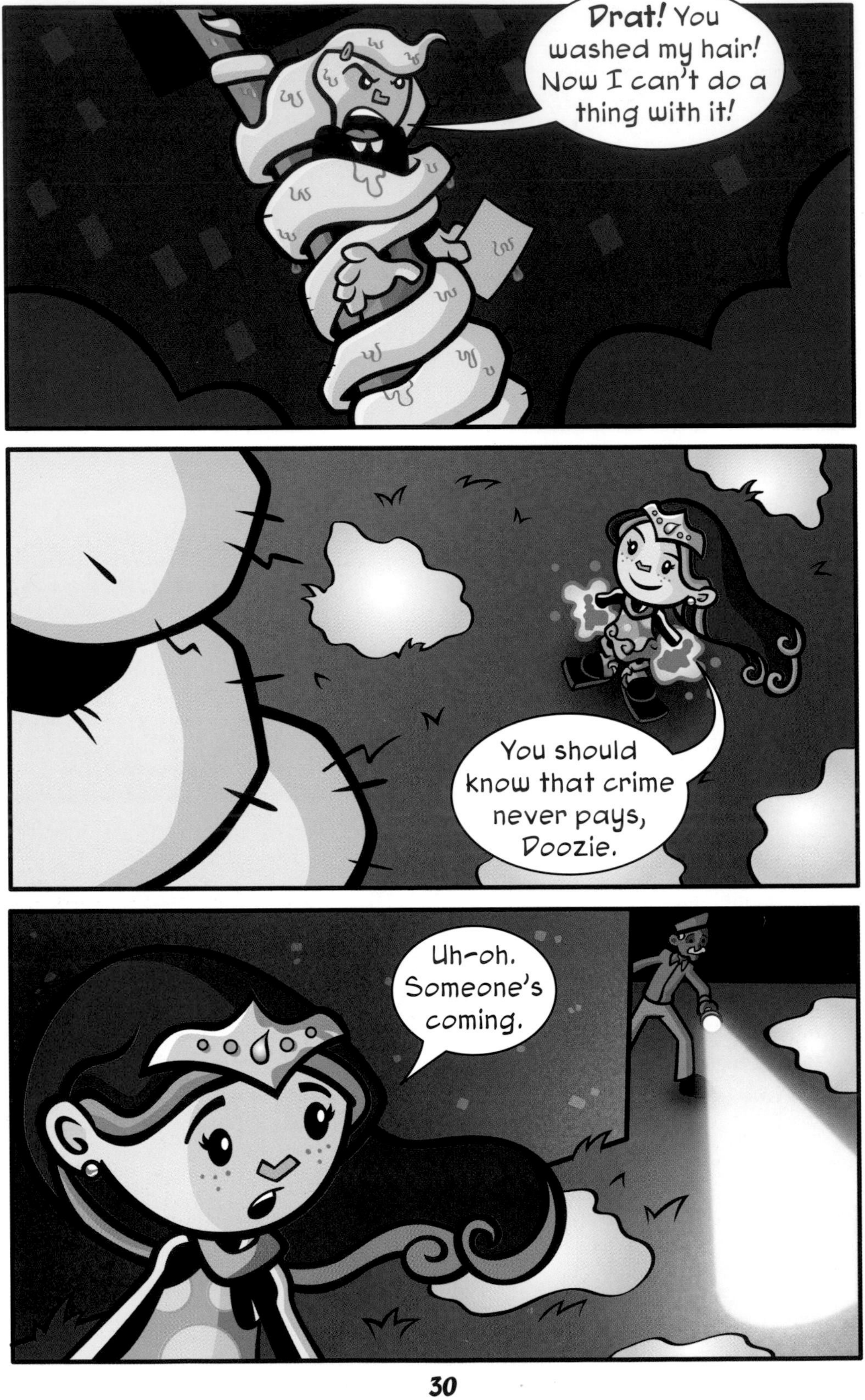
Drat! You washed my hair! Now I can't do a thing with it!
You should know that crime never pays, Doozie.
Uh-oh. Someone's coming.

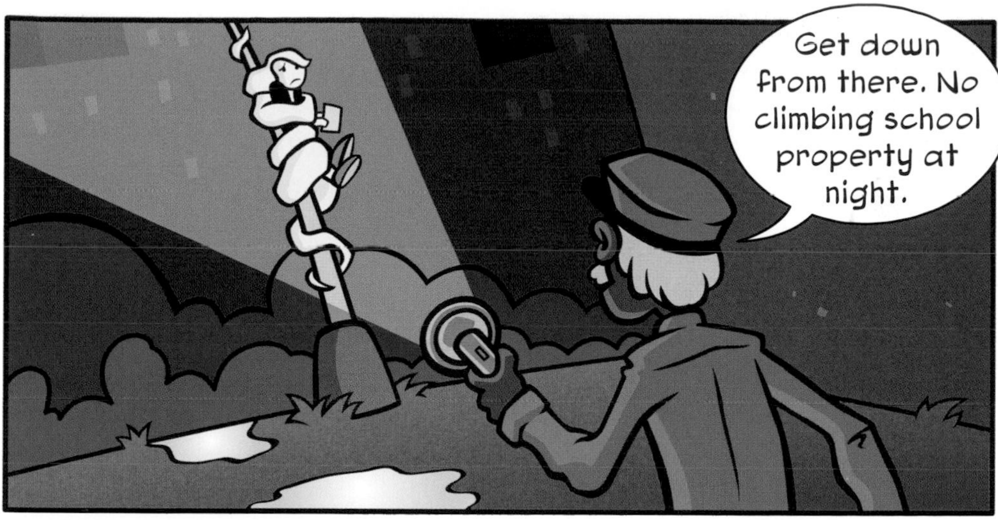
Get down from there. No climbing school property at night.

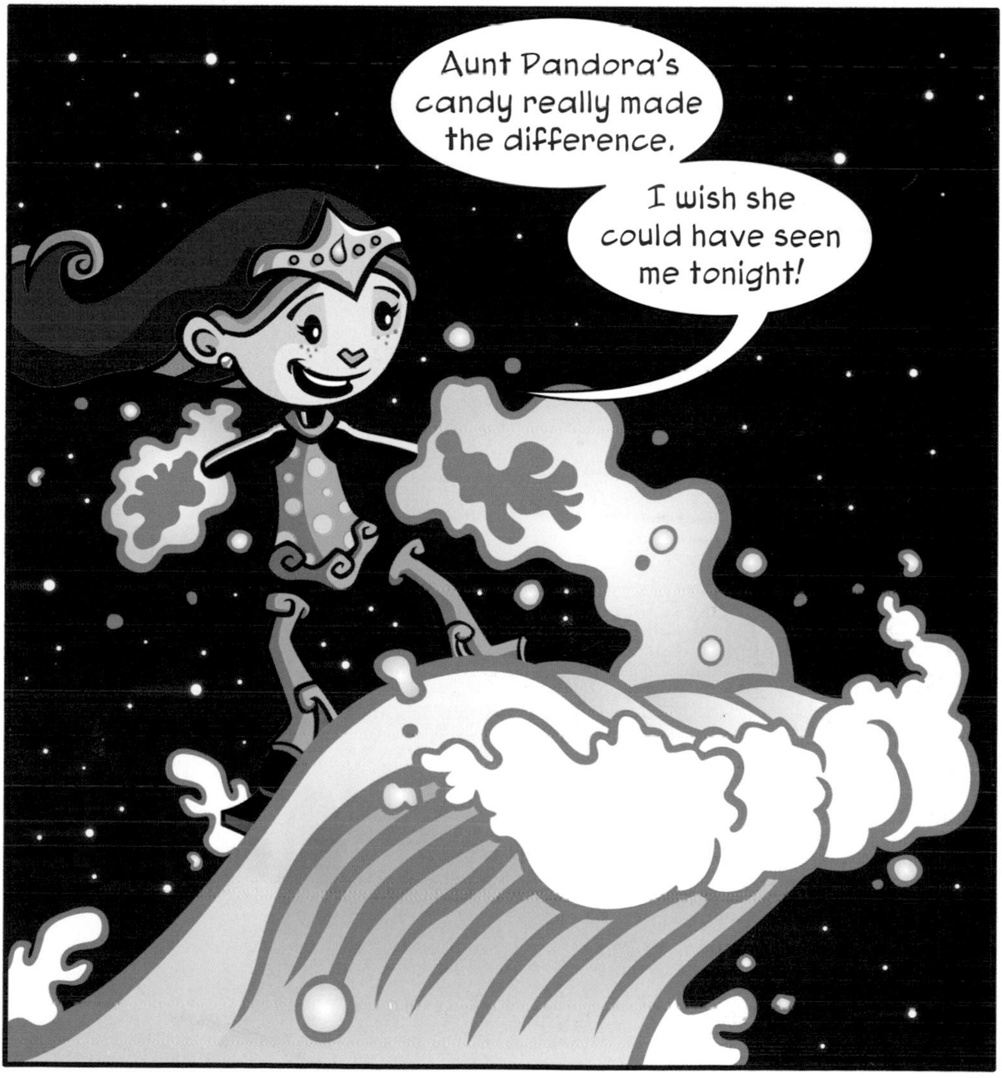
Aunt Pandora's candy really made the difference.
I wish she could have seen me tonight!

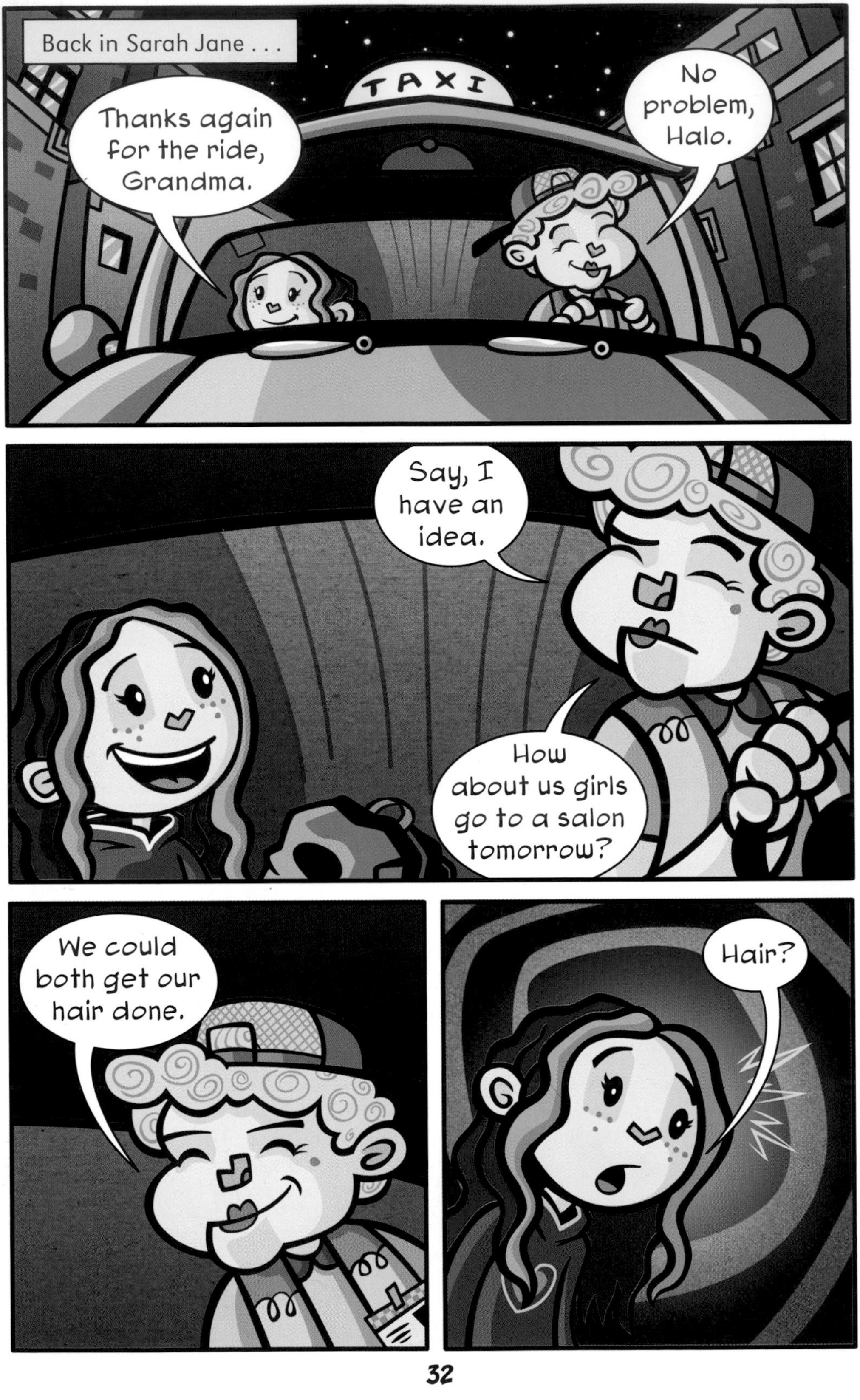
Back in Sarah Jane . . .
Thanks again for the ride, Grandma.
TAXI
No problem, Halo.
Say, I have an idea.
How about us girls go to a salon tomorrow?
We could both get our hair done.
Hair?

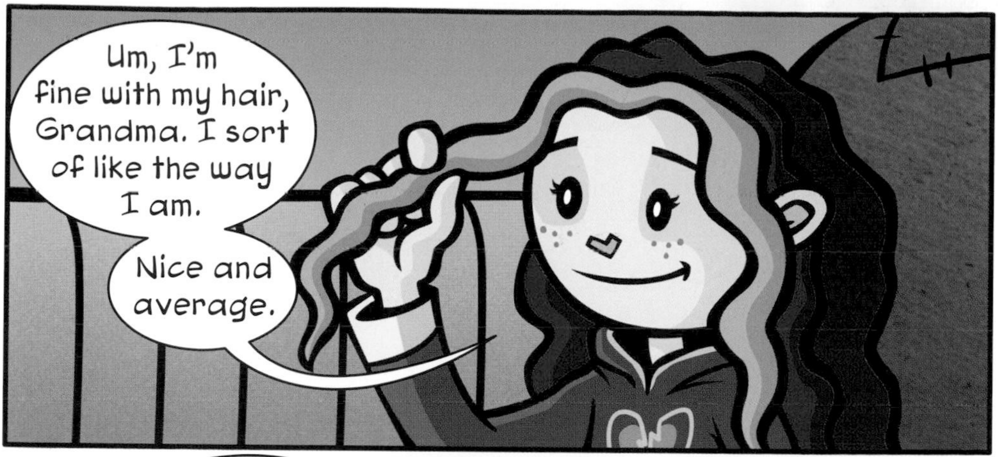
Um, I'm fine with my hair, Grandma. I sort of like the way I am.
Nice and average.

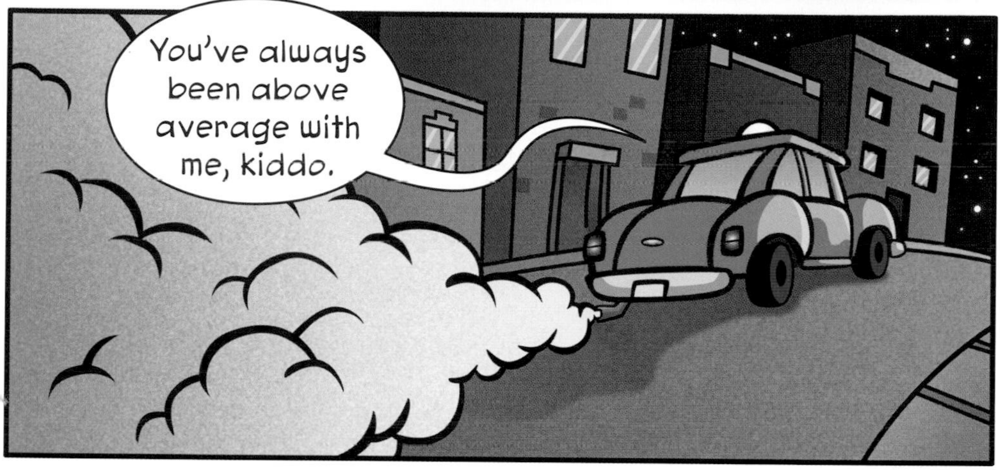
You've always been above average with me, kiddo.

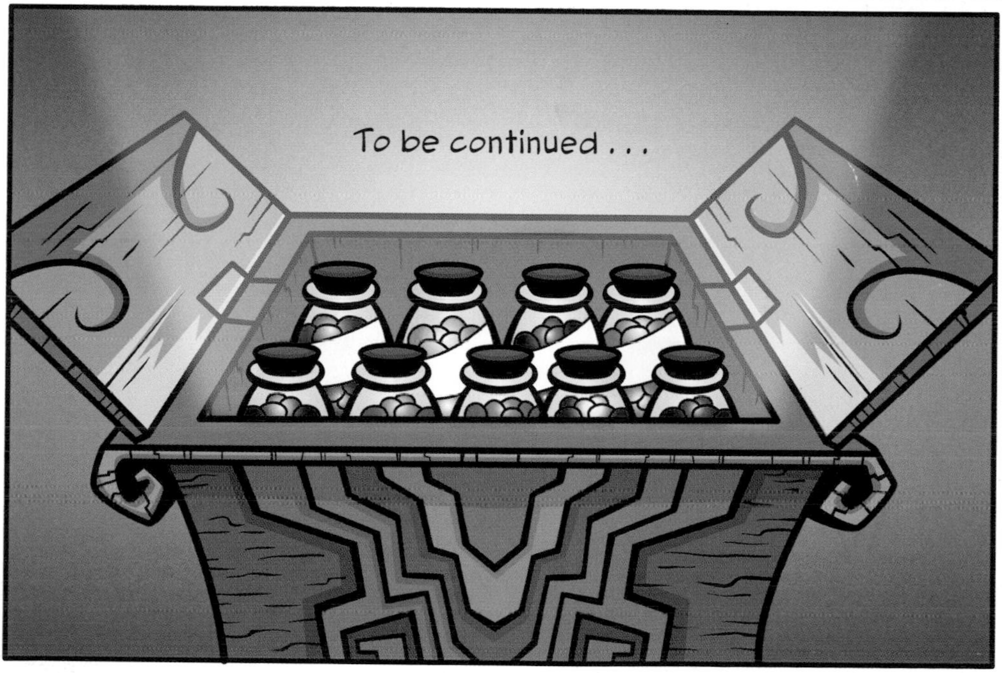
To be continued . . .

About The Author

Michael Dahl is the author of more than 200 books for children and young adults. He has won the AEP Distinguished Achievement Award three times for his non-fiction. His Finnegan Zwake mystery series was shortlisted twice by the Anthony and Agatha awards. He has also written the Library of Doom series and the Dragonblood books. He is a featured speaker at conferences around the country on graphic novels and high-interest books for boys.

About The Illustrator

Jeff Crowther has been drawing comics for as long as he can remember. Since graduating from college, Jeff has worked on a variety of illustrations for clients including Disney, Adventures Magazine, and Boy's Life Magazine. He also wrote and illustrated the webcomic Sketchbook and has self-published several mini-comics. Jeff lives in Boardman, Ohio, with his wife, Elizabeth, and their children, Jonas and Noelle.

Glossary

aqua (AH-kwah)—a Spanish word meaning "water"

average (AV-uh-rij)—usual, or ordinary

charcoal (CHAR-kole)—a form of carbon made from partially burned wood, often used as barbecue fuel

fuego (FWAY-go)—a Spanish word meaning "fire"

metropolis (meh-TRAH-poh-liss)—a large city

powerful (POU-ur-ful)—having great strength

pressure (PRESH-ur)—a burden or strain

property (PROP-ur-tee)—anything that is owned by an individual

salon (sah-LAHN)—a stylish business or shop

wisely (WIZE-lee)—to do something with good judgment

woozy (WOO-zee)—dizzy or mildly sick

Doozie Hiss

SUPER-VILLAIN

Villain Facts

First Appearance
Princess Candy: Sugar Hero

Real Name...............Medusa Marie Hiss

Occupation......................Honor Student

Height..............................4 feet 5 inches

Weight....................................75 pounds

Eyes..Black

Hair.....................Green (and snake-like)

Special Powers
Super-annoying personality; ability to instantly transform into a teacher's pet; living hair with deadly tentacle powers

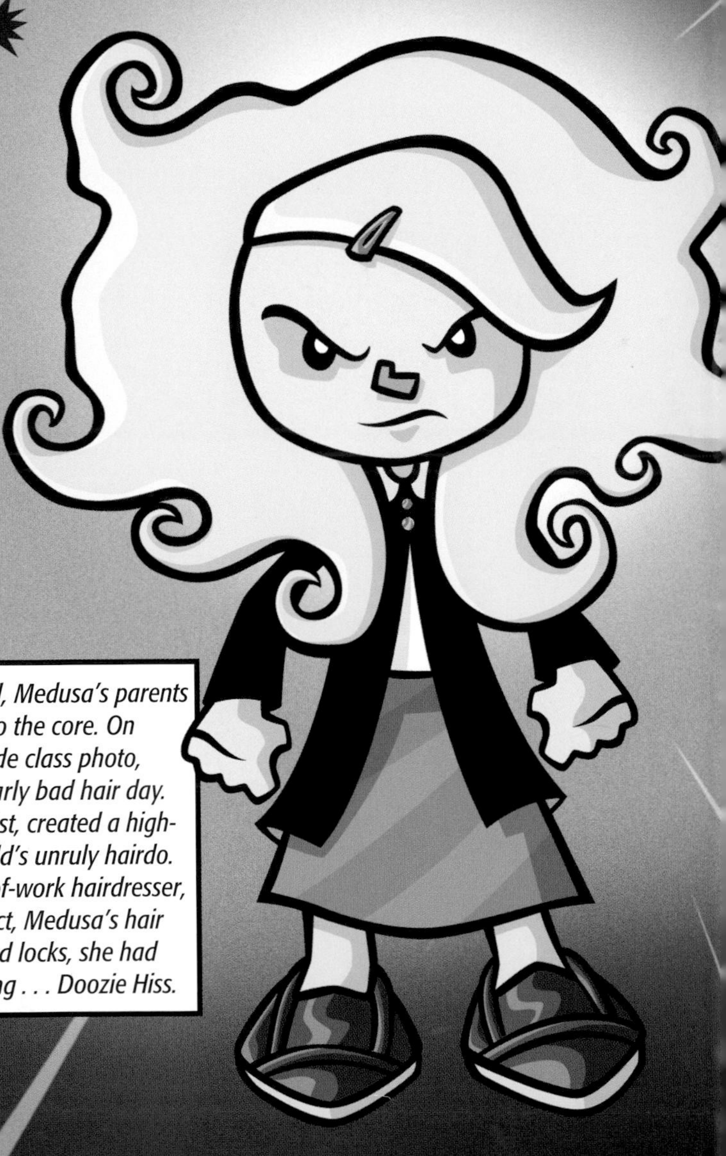

Unable to have another child, Medusa's parents spoiled their only daughter to the core. On the morning of her third-grade class photo, Medusa awoke to a particularly bad hair day. Her mother, a genetic scientist, created a high-tech hair gel to tame her child's unruly hairdo. But after her father, an out-of-work hairdresser, applied the prototype product, Medusa's hair turned deadly. With her lizard locks, she had become the evil and annoying . . . Doozie Hiss.

Princess Puzzlers

Q: Where does the word "candy" come from?

A: The word "candy" comes from the Arabic word "qandi," which means "sugar."

Q: Who discovered chocolate?

A: People from the ancient cultures of Mexico and Central America made chocolate more than 2,000 years ago.

Q: Which state produces the most chocolate?

A: Pennsylvania makes more chocolate than any other state. It is home to the Hershey chocolate factory.

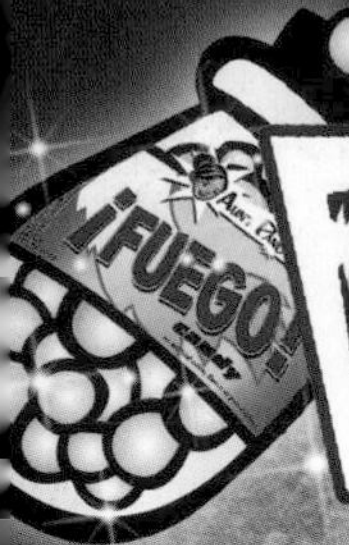
¡FUEGO!
candy

Discussion Question

1. Halo caught Doozie Hiss stealing the answers to a test. What do you think Doozie's punishment should be? Explain your answer.

2. Why do you think Aunt Pandora chose to give Halo the superpowered candy? What do you think she wanted Halo to do with them?

3. When she eats a piece of candy, Halo gains some amazing superpowers. If you could have just one superpower, what would it be? Explain.

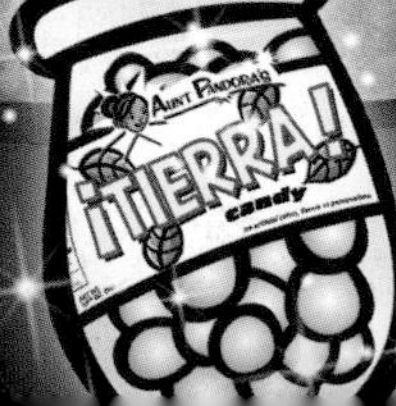
AUNT PANDORA'S
¡TIERRA!
candy

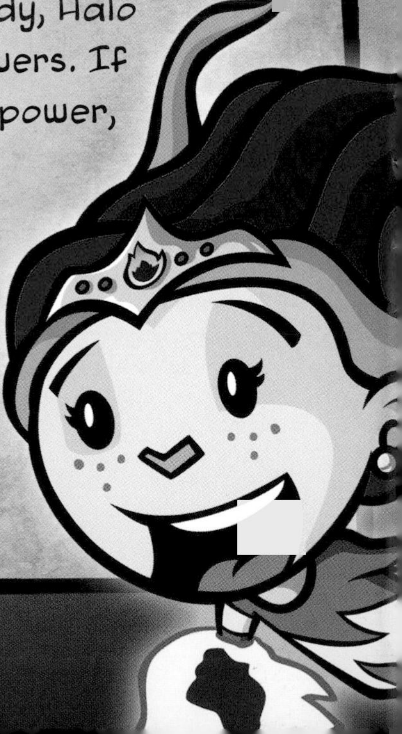

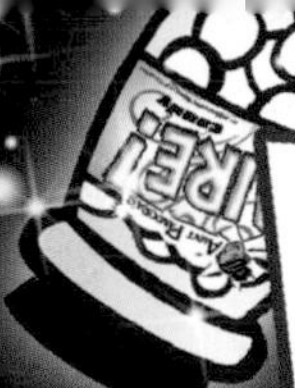

Writing Prompts

1. Think about your favorite candy. Now imagine that sweet treat could turn you into a superhero. Write about what you would do with your newfound powers.

2. At the end of the story, Halo leaves Doozie tied to the flagpole. Pretend you are the author and write a story about what happens next. Does Doozie escape? Is she punished for her crime?

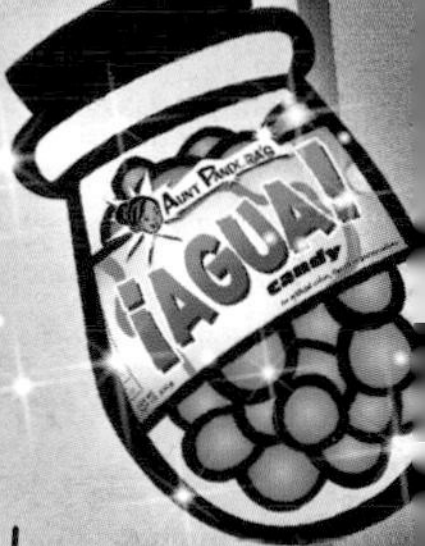
¡AGUA!
candy

3. Write your own Princess Candy comic. What kind of candy will Halo try next time? What super-villlain will she face? Use your imagination.

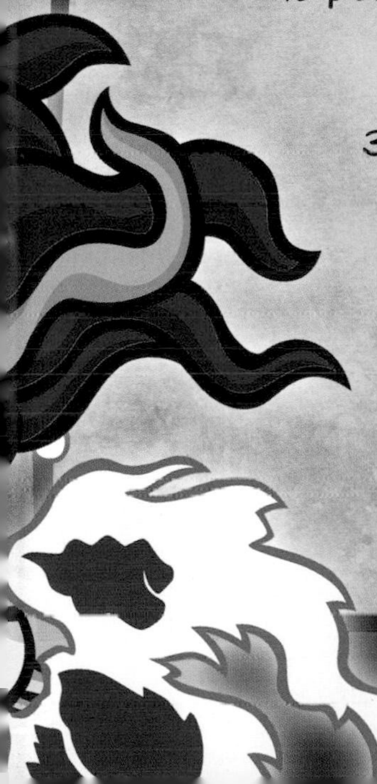

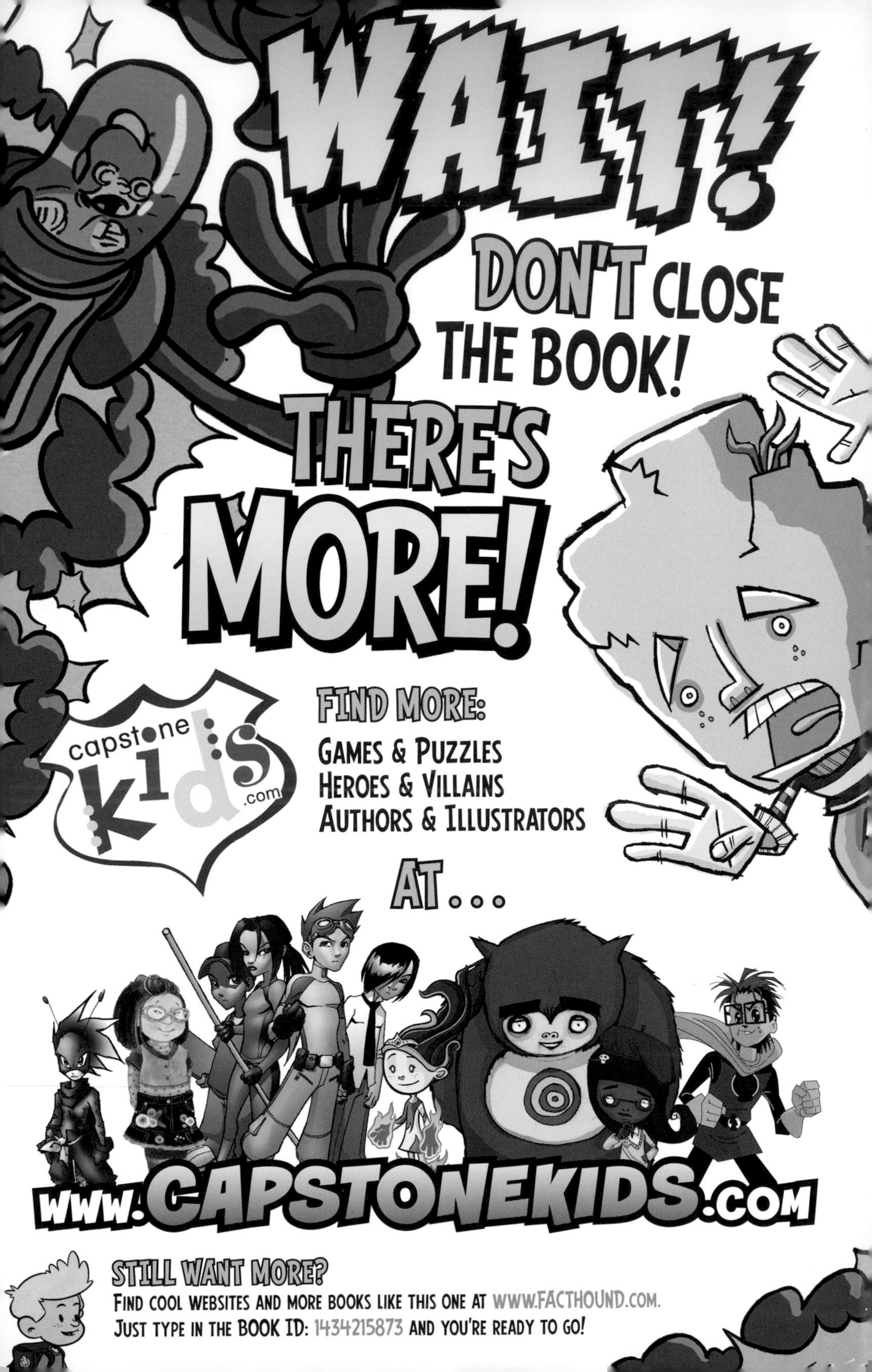
WAIT!
DON'T CLOSE THE BOOK!
THERE'S MORE!
capstone kids .com
FIND MORE:
GAMES & PUZZLES
HEROES & VILLAINS
AUTHORS & ILLUSTRATORS
AT...
WWW.CAPSTONEKIDS.COM
STILL WANT MORE?
FIND COOL WEBSITES AND MORE BOOKS LIKE THIS ONE AT WWW.FACTHOUND.COM.
JUST TYPE IN THE BOOK ID: 1434215873 AND YOU'RE READY TO GO!